Thomas M. Nealeigh
grew up performing with his
parents' travelling theatrical
troupe. Based in Hollywood,
he now runs FreakShow Deluxe
– a carnival-style sideshow
troupe. Nealeigh also works as a
performer, actor, writer, director,
producer and designer within the
entertainment industry; his plays
have been produced all over the
United States.

IN THE SAME SERIES

See You On The Backlot

THOMAS NEALEIGH

See You On The Backlot
THOMAS NEALEIGH

Series Editor: Peter Lancett

Published by Ransom Publishing Ltd.
51 Southgate Street, Winchester, Hampshire SO23 9EH, UK
www.ransom.co.uk

ISBN 978 184167 718 7

First published in 2009
Copyright © 2009 Ransom Publishing Ltd.
Cover by Flame Design, Cape Town, South Africa

A CIP catalogue record of this book is available from the British Library.
The right of Thomas Nealeigh to be identified as the author of this Work
has been asserted by him in accordance with sections 77 and 78 of the
Copyright, Design and Patents Act 1988.

Dedicated to my family:
Alice, Grennan and Charlotte.
To my Mum and Dad, thanks for
giving me the freedom to lead an
interesting life.

Special thanks to:
Wayne N. Keyser and James
Taylor, for their amazing
resources of carny and sideshow
lingo; Aye Jaye, for sharing true
stories about his life on the lot
with me; also John Robinson
and the fantastic resources of
SideShowWorld.com.

And of course, much thanks
to the many, many sideshow
performers I have had the
opportunity to meet and work
with over the years.

CHAPTER 1

So most nights I take time for cutting up the jackpot with some of the old-timers on the backlot. Usually after a quick stop by a grab joint, I head over to the G-Top to catch up on how the midway spun out for everyone. Always got to see if it's been a red date.

Sorry, I forgot. You're just a First of May, aren't you? Nights like these I just get going so much that I forget anything else but the midway. You probably didn't understand a word of what I was saying. Don't worry – I'll make sure I fill you in with what I mean as I go along, so just stick with me, right? You need to understand that this is no fireball show, right? Everything is on the level. Well, as much as it can be, anyway. You see, it's Big Mike – he runs this outfit – he don't take no truck to gimmicks or gaffs – that's anything fake – as far as the game joints are concerned. We ain't no Sunday school, but our front end runs pretty legit. Even if he could get away with it – and he could, with all the bagman pays out – he wouldn't do it. I've seen him set a goon squad on some crooked flattie, and give 'em the ole DQ, in other words, kick them off the lot. Shows are another thing though – he doesn't mind bouncers or dings (fake mummies and that sort of thing) with the working acts. Besides, he figures having them keeps the do-gooders off our backs.

OK now, hold up there, greenie. I can see by the way you're eyeing at me you don't know what I'm talking about. You're a real gazoonie, ain't you? Well, I don't have time for any gilly tagging along on our boards, so listen up and listen good. Until you get a circuit under your belt, that's a season on the road with us, stay out of the G-Top – that's the gambling tent – strictly for carnies only. If you think you know cards or can gamble pretty good, nothing will fix that quicker than playing one of the games going on in there. Trust me, son, any agent worth his weight will have you stuck in a build-up faster than I can turn a tip – you know, pull in a mark and take money off him. I've seen it happen – before you know it, you've gambled away your whole bankroll and got nothing but the bare walls of the bunkhouse for company... assuming you can even keep that! Otherwise you're scrambling for some place on the boards or you'll have to carry the banner. Um... that means you'll be sleeping under someone's truck or under a canvas tent.

Keep up with me, now – not all of this will make sense right away! But stick with me, kid, and I'll tell you everything you need to know.

Listen here, back-yard boy, I want you to understand that you are talking to the one and only 'Clown Prince of the Sideshow'! That's the handle the other carnies have given me over the past few years, but you can call me Tony. My pops, Charlie, owns the Ten-in-One you signed on for. Ten acts – One show. Pops says we come right down the line from some famous circus folks – but that don't buy us any respect from anyone here. Well, it does, but not as much as the roll we have by the end of each night we're on the circuit.

Money's what it's all about, right? We're well-respected by Big Mike and the other carnies here – that's why you always find our show at First Call, the best location on the lot, without a crescent in our banner line, meaning we get the space to unfurl our banner straight. We help get the townies in the gate and pull them all the way through to the back end. We're known for giving the marks a great time with our Boston Version – that's the best version of our show we can do – before they head out into the rest of the carnival... *and* we don't take all their money under our top, so they still have plenty to spend on the rest of the midway. Everyone appreciates that.

Some pitchmen and talkers, they're not happy if a mark leaves their joint with even a dime in their pockets - but my pops and I, we understand how it works. You always need to leave a mooch a dollar for gas, that's what my pops says. We do right by the other people on the lot, and they do right by us. And you'd better, too, if you're going to be on the road with us. Around here there's no time to be cleaning up after a milk baby, you know? Since this is the first season you've ever signed up for, you're a 'First of May'. That means you're what we call 'green help', a 'greenhorn' or 'gazoonie.' So I'm going to be calling you those names until you're with it.

And see, 'with it' is what you want to be. When you're with it, you're educated, you understand how the carnival works, so no one can take advantage of you – and you can help watch everyone else's backs, too. We look out for each other here. There's no one else but us – this is our world! From one end of the midway to the other, through the backlot and back yard, front end to back end. Rides, games, shows, single-os – shows with just one attraction – grease joints where a mark can get a bite to eat... each and every single agent, pitchman, talker, jock and act needs to make their nut, you know, the cost of just paying everything it takes to run your show, to stay on the road. And there is no place for us but the road. No other place for us to go. No other way to make any money. I mean, what else could some of these guys do? Go straight?

Why, my pops and I have been on the road since I can remember! We've got sawdust in our blood. I don't think I've ever slept in a bunk that wasn't bolted to the floor – and spent more than a couple nights carrying the banner, too. Oh! Wait, hold on...

See that girl over there? The one standing by the show tent? No, no – not the girl on the bally stage, where you shout your pitch to get the townies into your show... I'm pointing to the one at the ticket box over there. That's my Delilah. She's a bit sweet on me, and I won't take to anyone having any beef with her. You want some girlie of your own? Well, sure you do! It gets lonely on the lot, sometimes. You should have no trouble finding one. Maybe you'll get some townie at each spot, or maybe a girl on the circuit – or even some lot lizard if you get desperate enough. I heard from some guys that they have a girl in every town on the circuit. Some guys even have a couple of wives along the way! You'd think they were movie stars, the way they talk. Not for me, though. Oh no, there's only one girl for me – and that's Delilah. Sometimes I could just stand here all day watching her... but we've got to get going if I'm going to show you all around.

Now this is front end. Every place you see a grease joint – that's concessions – and they make good money if they do it right. And they're always considered front end, no matter where they are. We have games up through here – punk joints, flat stores, bendovers and all the rest. Call them whatever you want – they are all games – and most of them are covered in garbage and paste (you don't think we'd spend a lot on prizes do you? We're here to make a buck), anything to keep the mooches coming and dropping a wad at trying to win a cheap little prize. This is where a good agent, the guy who runs the game, can really rake in the bucks – especially from townies on their way out after the shows. Some of those hayseeds just never want the night to end!

Now we need to wrap up this little tour, so let's keep moving. This is the back end. Here's where most of the rides are: your flat rides – flatties – for the kiddies, chump-twisters (those ones will rough the change right out of your pockets), plus a few of the bigger ones for the adults. And then some dark rides, like the tunnel of love or a haunted house. Then over next to them is where the real big shows are, because it helps draw the crowds through the whole carnival – spending their money as they go – and on their way back through to get out, too. You have to have a great banner line to make the marks take notice. See over there, how each of those big banners says what acts the rubes can expect to see once they're in the joint? You have the Ten-in-Ones (freak shows), magic shows, girly shows (that's where you can meet a fine girl, if you want), crime and drug abuse shows (showing the horrors of an illegal life), then a tableau or two (just model villages and things to look at), depending on where we are. There's also single-os, then the museums, grind and ding shows (where it's a 'free' show that they make you pay to get *out* of), animal shows and baby shows. We're lucky on this circuit because Big Mike has a good mix of live working acts and freak shows, and that keeps the citizens coming through the gate. And the circuit knows Big Mike – they know he's never burned a lot or caused a beef with the locals – so I think we get a better deal than most. All I know is it brings out the citizens to see our show.

We have to hurry – it's almost time for the shows to start!

Behind the shows and rides is the back yard. It's the living lot where the jocks and carnies keep house. Donnikers are over there – that's the toilets. Over there's the private trailers and tents for those who can afford them, and bunkhouses for those who can't – that's where you're going to be. Don't forget to keep your valuables locked up, if you got any. The carnies look out for each other, but there's still them that'll rob you blind if they need a hook-up or have lost their bankroll at the G-Top or something. You might want to think about getting a grouch bag to keep your stuff while you're on the midway. Then right over there's the showers, if the water's working. Right here's the cook shack, if you want to eat. You *should* eat here, too, rather than out on the midway with the rubes at a grab joint. Less expensive... and better food, too! If you keep in good with the management, they may even extend a bit of credit if you find yourself short.

Me? A carny?! No, no... not me. I'm a showman, son. You'll see once the night starts. Carnies, they're the ride and food jocks, the canvas men, pitchmen and agents, too. You'll be one once you're with it – if you last the season. But being in the show – *that* is being with it in a whole other way! Here, come back onto the midway with me and I'll show you.

Do me a favour, will you? Don't say 'midway' when you're around the carnies,

OK? It's something my pops says, but it's really from back when the circus had sideshows with it. Nowadays, most of the chumps will go to an arena or something to see a circus. All they care about is animals and high-wire acts. There's no room for us there any more. Circus doesn't care – they call us 'kid shows', you know? They've got squeaky-clean gags and shows and clowns – no room for a grift or girly show. Seems like no one wants to see freaks any more, either. Well, I mean, that's what I hear the people saying – but we never have any problems bringing in the bucks at the big shows. Thing is, there just aren't that many true freaks any more. Most of these guys in the sideshows are working acts and gaff what they do – in other words, they use make-up or prosthetics – or have stuff done to themselves so they can call themselves freaks. Even then they still need to be working acts. Good thing we have Big Mike. He cares about us, you know?

Anyway...

Look – just forget I told you any of that, all right? I have to get ready for the show. You want to see why they call me the 'Clown Prince' right? Well, in about an hour you're going to see me hanging upside-down from that crane over there. It cost a bit to get that thing, let me tell you, but Pops insists that we'll bring in so much from this stunt that we'll more than make up for the up-front money.

So, here's the stunt. See, I'm going to be tied up in this straightjacket, with these chains wrapped around me and then all these padlocks locked through the chains, too. That's where you come in. You're my shill for this gag, my 'inside man' to help me sell this to the yokels. That's why I didn't give you one of our show's shirts or anything, so you don't stand out. You just wear your street duds and, when I'm pulling volunteers out of the crowd, you just have to make sure to get yourself where I can see you. It will probably be best if you stand right next to the hawker – that's the guy selling refreshments – who'll be walking through the crowd right then. Remember, you have to pretend you've never seen anything like this before. You're going to make sure no funny business happens with the buckles of the straightjacket, and then double-check the chain gets wrapped around me and the padlocks fastened the way we went over it earlier, right? Pops will be checking to make sure the ankle harness is set the way it is supposed to be – and I know I can trust him – but I want you to double-check everything he does. Just don't make it look like you're checking up on him, OK?

Then after I'm up in the air, leave it up to me. Big stunt like that will bring the crowds running to our tent – the lot man, who's the guy who owns the grounds, and Big Mike have been setting this up with the papers and press, so there should be a lot of people here to see it. Then be ready, OK? Because once I'm out of the jacket and chains, Charlie (that's my pops, remember?) is going to look to clear the midway when he turns the tip – that's getting the people in – into our show. After that, just keep close, because we're going to run the grind – in other words, go through the show – like there's no tomorrow. Like I said, Charlie will be the outside talker – and there's none better when he's on his game – then Murphy will be the inside talker and getting the acts through the grind. We're lucky, we already have a bender and fakir, and I can do some work with fire and a few other things – and then we have another couple of working acts to round out the show. Between the blade box and the blow-off, we'll make our nut, even a little more if we do an after-catch – that's selling them some slum (junk or something else) once they're inside.

So your job, as Charlie makes the pitch to turn the tip, is to be one of the first to step up to the monkey box and buy a ticket. Head right on in like you can hardly wait to see the show – and the rubes will follow in right behind you. Once you're in you go on through and exit out the back. Don't forget to come back around front and do the whole thing over again – buy another ticket and walk through! We'll be running the bally all night, so you can be sure we're going to need you every show. Last kid in your place ended up wandering off in the middle of a night and leaving us short – so try to keep it together, OK? Remember, you don't get paid until after we count out at the end of the night. I know it's hard not to get caught up in everything going on, but you're working here, now… and there's a lot of work to do.

I mean – look at me. If you saw me outside of the lights here, you'd think I was just another dumb punk, wouldn't you? Not even old enough to shave, not old enough to drive. Don't let it fool you, son. I may not be able to shave, but I can drive any one of these trucks. I can set up a two hundred foot banner line in the rain practically by myself, then remember every dead man, that's the pegs that hold the banner lines and those holding up the top, when we pull up stakes to make the jump to the next town. I can bally with the best of them and turn a tip almost as fast as my pops. I know which marks to go for and which make too much heat. I can keep a beef under our awnings and BC – that's Be Cool – when I need to. That's why I'm the Prince of the Sideshow, greenie, and why you're a First of May. Don't you worry none, though – you stick by me and I'll make sure that you're with it by the end of the season, all right?

OK, it's time. You still have the carny roll I gave you? Looks like a big roll of bills, right? Only it's just a few bills wrapped around paper to make it look good. Keep it close – and use that cash to front your way into the show. Watch out for grifters – con artists – and pickpockets. Remember – you're one of us, now. If you do well today, there will be plenty more to do tomorrow... See you on the backlot!

CHAPTER 2

What do you think of that, gazoonie? Another red date down! Tonight's show was quite the draw – it seemed like the top was always full and the midway always clear. We turned tips one right after another, then it seemed like everyone wanted to pay to see the blade box up close and *still* drop a dime for the blow-off! Whew – nights like this wear me out. So once the lights are off and the crowds have gone home... I take some time for myself to pal around the lot before heading back to our top.

Most nights I cut the jackpot – talk – with some of the old-timers, after stopping at a grab joint. Tonight is different, though.

See You On The Backlot

Some of the carnies have been talking about some old friends hoboing around who were coming through the lot – so I wanted the chance to hear their stories. Not just some yarns, I mean the real deal. That's what cutting the jackpot is, sharing stories. Most of the old guys who've been on the circuit a while have something to say that's really worth listening to. Even my old pops, when he's deep in his cups, has a few things to tell everyone that are worth sticking around for.

But tonight was a total disappointment as far as I'm concerned. Instead of shooting the bull with the greatest carnies in the world, all I found was two old tosspots, pissing in the wind and trying to get high off of whatever juice anyone would throw at them. They didn't have no stories to tell or anything to share that was worth my time. I don't think they were real carnies at all – since they couldn't even speak a word of ciazarn (that pig-latin kind of code the carnies use that I've been trying to teach you). Then on top of that, after a few drinks one of them starts in on me about my show.

Starts going on about how 'in my day we would never do this...' or 'a real carny would do this instead...' then rambles on about taking chumps and burning lots and complaining how everyone is working too hard and how they used to do it so they never had to do any work.

Sorry if I'm being rude, but those old rummies make me so mad. It's bad enough I blow my pipes getting the words out to the huge crowds I got coming to see us. I can barely talk to these guys because of it, so it makes it hard to step up when they start talking about my da. They don't know my pops. They don't know me. I could tell the other carnies were getting uncomfortable when those old bums started talking stuff about what happened to my mum and how they think my pops is running our show into the ground. That's why I left... I don't need that kind of...

Well, anyways, I need to get back to look over the receipts and do a last count. Pops always handles it, but I feel better if I can get an idea about how much the show is really bringing in. Now I realise you're probably wondering how we make our money, what with all the shorting and dings that come with running our show. It kind of goes like this:

Pops rents our space on the midway from Big Mike for the run of the location. Big Mike runs the carnival fence to fence – so we never have the problems of an independent midway, where some idiot locals with a booth might end up having a beef and giving our whole show a bad name. Everyone's in competition with each other on our midway, sure – I mean, if someone else takes a dollar out of a yokel's pocket, that's one less dollar *we* can take – but Big Mike likes to keep it friendly between all the concessions and shows. Guess he figures everyone's got a stake in making sure the whole carnival does well. Anyways, those who can't cut it tend not to show at the next location. Sometimes Pops says Big Mike is living in the past, thinking that folks these days will come out to a carnival filled with so many ways to take them for as much money as possible. He says people would rather watch television or movies than leave their houses. That if they want entertainment they'll head to a theme park or spend an afternoon watching elephants in an air-conditioned arena, rather than come out to a carnival. Pops says that these days ain't nothing compared with what it used to be like, back in what he calls the 'salad days'.

I don't understand that saying. Never have. Something old people say to each other I guess. Doesn't matter, either. All that matters is that without Big Mike we don't have a show. And no show means no money.

Anyways – along with renting the space, there's always these other dings. Dings are expenses the greenies don't count on, like extra insurance, cut-ins (that's hooking us up to the genny – the generator on the Light Truck – so we can have electricity for our top), parking for the trucks, maybe some special IDs or other nonsense the lot has cooked up to get some extra cash from everyone. Then if they decide to do some Dollar Day or other special, we lose our shirts on top of that... Well we just have to take it, because by the time we find out about it, it's too late to pass off on the place and find a new place to stake. A show like ours doesn't do well barnstorming – that's when we set up somewhere with no notice. We need a carnival on a lot to make our nut.

Then there's the payoffs, too. It doesn't matter how clean our show is, some local politician or sheriff is always standing there with their hand out to help get us through an inspection or some such. Usually there's a patch, one of the carnies, who takes care of all that by making 'donations'... but sometimes it doesn't matter. Sometimes there's a do-gooder in a town who decides that all carnivals are nothing but rip-off games, with flat joints – that's a rigged game set-up – and the like, or immoral, with the freak or girly shows. Or even worse, cruel to animals – as if there were any animals with us that couldn't hold their own if they needed to. And I've never known any animal show that was really cruel to any creature in its care. Well, if some townie just decides he wants to squeeze our teats, then that is just what he's going to do until he gets wet. It is easier to pay them off just to leave us alone. Shoot, most of the mooches WANT to be ripped off! They expect it – that's part of the reason they're here in the first place.

All right where was I? OK, so once we're through paying out for all that just to set up, we might find out we have to drop off banners at the end of our line because we were shorted space. Maybe, if it's not too much space we've lost, we can crescent – which means we bend our banner line – just to get it all up there. It doesn't look as good, though. And this show is all about looking good. That's what my pops says, anyways.

That all matters, of course, because we have to pay out to the head office – that's Big Mike – for every ticket we sell. The office has people all over the lot, checking on numbers and making sure no one is shorting the house. What we get left after all that is our end. That and what we sell inside. See, that money they *know* we're getting, but they don't know how much, so we can keep some back before the first count.

Of course, we're not only taking the marks' money at the door! Once the rubes are under the canvas, we got a few more ways to shake a couple bucks out of them. About halfway through we bring out our bender, Bettie – that's the contortionist girl you saw up on the bally – in a skimpy costume, and she gets into the blade box. Now once she's inside, she hands her costume out of one of the holes on the top to Murphy, the talker. Then he slides all these blades through the box, leaving them sticking in there while the girl is bending her body around in the box to keep from being impaled. See, once all the blades are in, the talker invites the men to come up and see the girl in the box, now without her costume. We tell them that she only gets the money they give, so they have to pay a dollar to come up and look. When they look through, they see that she's in a bikini she had hidden under her costume – but by then they've already paid their money!

Then, at the end of the show, our talker steps up to the curtain, close to the way out, and offers to let people step behind it for another dollar. Because, of course, back there, they'll see something even better!

No, no... nothing like Barnum's 'this way to the egress' gag, or tricking them into looking into a mirror or something. Not with any show that Charlie puts on! My pops, he went and got himself a real half-and-half... that's a half-man half-woman gag for this circuit. She's real nice. She told me she's using the money from this season to go all the way. I didn't ask her which direction she's going. Honestly, I was kind of disgusted with it. I mean – here she is with an honest way to make money, just letting the rubes look at her, and she doesn't have to say or do anything if she doesn't want to, but she wants to change. It must be her boyfriend who doesn't like people looking at her or something. I've seen him around and he looks like that type. I would never change for anyone... and I certainly don't want anyone changing for me!

I asked Pops about it, and he kinda laughed at me, which made me mad. But then he sat me down for a bit and began talking about being more understanding of other people, and keeping my mind open to other things. Honestly, I had stopped listening by that point. See, Charlie has been to college and stuff. One of the carnies asked me once why someone who's a doctor would run a Ten-in-One in some flea-bitten sideshow, but one of the other guys told him to shut his yapper and BC. I didn't see what the big deal was, you know, why that guy was telling him to Be Cool – but I was pretty young then. I asked Pops about it, but he didn't tell me anything; he just looked sad and wandered off. It took me a bit to understand that not every doctor is the medical kind. I'm still not sure what kind of doctor Charlie is, but he's the kind where I don't have to go to some school away from him. He spends some time teaching me every morning before things get busy. It's probably the best time of our day, because it's usually too early for him to have had a drink yet. Sometimes, though, he hasn't come sober from the night before.

So, anyway, it's the inside money that really helps pay everyone on the show. Of course, every time one of our people wanders off and never returns, or shorts *us* with the ticket money, or some bonehead makes a mistake that damages equipment or gets someone injured... well, that always seems to put us closer to disaster. That's why I need to get back to do a count before it gets much later, and Charlie decides to head over the G-Top.

You know the other day, Murphy – he's been with our show a while – he says to me, 'Boy – you don't need to be spendin' your time worryin' about such things. You should spend your time just being the kid you're supposed to be.'

Now I ask you, would *you* want to spend your time just being some punk? Stuck in some crummy school? Stranded in one place 'cause your da doesn't care enough to take care of you after your mum's gone? Sounds like something for the chumps, to me. Here, it's me and my pops all the way!

Besides, it's not like I'm the only one keeping an eye out for everything going on with the show. There's Murphy, who my da says has been with him since he started running the show. Murphy used to tell me about mum when I was younger – but at some point I guess Charlie asked him to stop doing it because he never said another word. Guess it was too sad for Charlie. Anyway, without Murphy there probably wouldn't be a show at all! Sure, Charlie is great – but I can't keep my eye on everything Charlie may have overlooked – and that's where Murphy comes in.

The rest of our crew, whether they're First of Mays, or on their one hundredth season, know enough to keep Charlie out of Big Mike's path whenever he's on a bender. Murphy told me once that Big Mike knows all about Charlie's late nights, but as long as he doesn't have to see it or put up with it, he will ignore it. At least so long as the show keeps making money.

And, luckily for us, the show makes a *lot* of money.

Of course, it's a lot of work. We're going to be pulling up stakes and making the jump to the next location day after tomorrow. There will be a lot more jumps after that, too. That's what the beans are for – they give some added pep to the workers, so we can make the long night after the show when we're tearing down the tent and loading the trucks before driving all night. And once we're there, we're going to have to set everything up before taking time to rest.

That's the best time, really, once we're in the air and ready to drop, especially if we're at a lot for a few days or a week. Then we can relax in the mornings – at least until the weekend comes, when we might run shows throughout the day as well as the night.

Look, it's getting late now, and we have a full day tomorrow before the jump. So let me get to my work before I turn in. Before I go, though, I want you to think about this: those old carnies, they think they're with it – but they're not. Me? I'm a showman.

It takes a lot more to sell a show than just framing it up. It takes real skill and talent to sell it to a crowd, otherwise any grinder could do it. On nights when Charlie isn't up for it, I take over as talker – sometimes inside and sometimes out – plus do my acts and keep my eye on the brass ring, too – you know, make sure that the take is good and that everything runs smoothly. I don't care what Murphy says... this is my life. This is what I do. I'm the 'Clown Prince of the Sideshow'.

And I intend to stay that way.

CHAPTER 3

FINALLY! Thank goodness you made it, gazoonie! I've been through more on this jump than I ever thought I'd have to.

Did you pick up what I asked you to? The cotton mop-head? The white gasoline? OK, great, thanks! Here, sit down with me for a minute and I'll tell you what happened, while I get these fire-eating torches together for tonight's show. Good thing you went with the advance man like I told you to last night. You ended up missing all the mess.

Ahh, just as well, I suppose. It was a jump like any of the hundred jumps we've done before. Not too close, not too far.

I mean sure, we're not forty-milers, but it's not as if we're heading to the ends of the earth. You know what I mean by forty-milers, or cake-eaters. What they do, see, is settle themselves down somewhere safe, then they just make the jumps out to the lots from wherever they are. Usually, it's within a single day's drive or so from where they live, which means they never travel more than forty miles or so from their home base. I mean they could go home every night if they wanted to! Why they would want to do anything like that I have no idea. Isn't that the fun? Being on the road? That would be kind of tough for me, I'll tell you that for nothing. The road is what I'm about.

Course, most of them aren't travelling with shows. Most of the time they're retirees who've got their cash invested in some chump-twister ride or something. Or got a stand that sells snacks. Then they have their snotty grandkids and those kids' even-more-snotty friends working it during the summer season. I hate those kids. They act like they're so much better than us. But they all seem the same, lot after lot after lot.

Those kids. God, I hate them! They don't understand what we're doing. They don't understand the history, the past – or the future of what I'm doing here. They're not 'with it'. If another one of them ever looks at Delilah again, I swear…

But back to the forty-milers. We couldn't be a forty-miler show, even if we wanted to. Who would want to see us? Honestly? We'd never get far enough away to bring in new audiences. Charlie got me to understand that, pretty quickly; we would see the same crowds over and over. And then those crowds would get tired of seeing the same show over and over again. The only way to keep the townies coming, Charlie says, would be to offer something new each time we came through.

Normally, I just shut Charlie out when he gets into rambling. But when he was telling me all this, it got me to thinking. Who would we get as performers? I mean, a bender or fakir – like we have now – might be OK. Work out new acts and get new skills, and the rubes can see the same performer time and again. But someone like our half-and-half, a fat lady or one of those wolf-boys – well, they wouldn't be able to do more than one set of shows with us. Once a group has seen the blow-off, would they really pay to see it, again?

OK, so I was telling you what happened on the jump before I got sidetracked. Well, usually I run most of the things once we start breaking down, because once Charlie gets things started up, well, he has other things he needs to handle, right? Right!

But this time there's something else up. I don't know why, but Charlie won't get off our backs through the entire teardown. That's never good, because there's so much to do! I know that he thinks he knows everything – but he doesn't. He may have started this show, but Murphy tells me he hasn't slung canvas in years. I mean, why should he? That's what he has me for.

I know the routine.

I know how it fits together.

I *know* the fastest way to get it broken down and loaded up so we can get on the road!

But when Charlie gets it into his head that he's got a faster way of doing things, he sits on top of us. And something always goes wrong.

So let me tell you how it works on the last night on a particular lot. Once the last show of the night is done, almost before the last of the rubes leave the grounds, everyone's already breaking the whole carnival down. As soon as we kick the stragglers out of the top, we start pulling the canvas and breaking down the frame. Not all of us, of course. Some of the performers are 'delicate,' as Murphy says. Of course, there are still plenty of props to be loaded up, and the banner line needs to come down. If the weather's good though, the banner line will come down while the last show is still on. That was my idea – it always saves us some time.

Why time is important is because Big Mike never lets us spend a night in a spot if we're not opening there the next night. After all – every day on the lot is another day that has to be paid for, right? So we break it down and head out to the next spot right away after we're done.

Sometimes, if the jump's a little longer, we stop at a motel on the way. Sometimes Pops would let me choose where we'd stay. While our performers would be finding their own way in their campers or whatever, it'd just be Charlie and me on our rig together. Charlie always seemed to like it better when I'd find these really out of the way places – and I mean *way* off the beaten track. Sometimes he'd let me choose names for us to register under, too. Not something boring like our real names! So, instead of being Charlie and Tony Grice, we'd use all of my names instead. So we'd register as Charles and Richard Anthony (cause, you know, my name's Richard Anthony Grice). Or we'd be Chuck and Dick Cloonie or something. Pops always laughed at that one – not just at calling me 'Dick' – but because 'Cloonie' is a version of 'Clownie' or 'Carnie'. He's a strange one, Charlie.

Anyway, we'd get registered, then order in pizzas and stuff, and watch movies on the television from under tents we made on the beds out of the covers. I'm getting too old for that kid stuff, now – but those are some of my best memories with my da. I don't ever remember him really drinking a lot when we were at the motels, either.

But back to now. This time we weren't planning a stopover; Murphy was riding with us, so he and Charlie would split the driving on the overnight run. By that I mean that Murphy and I would split the driving, while Charlie slept it off on the pallet behind the seats.

But Charlie wouldn't get off our backs! Every time I turned around he had told someone to do something different from what I had told them to do – so everything was a mess! It seemed like forever to get it all broken down. By the time we were loaded up in the trucks, all the rest of the carnival was on the road. Good thing I had thought to send you with the advance man, so you could make sure our spot was staked

out. We were the last ones to leave the lot
– like a bunch of chumps!

I was pretty steamed, let me tell you.
Then, of course, Charlie was in no shape
to drive and Murphy was just worn out.
And so was I. Finally, we just had to pull
over, so that Murphy and I could sleep
some. That's what made us late getting to
the lot here. We finally got here, long after
everyone else, and I could tell Big Mike
was mad because our stake wasn't in a
prime spot.

Don't worry, gazoonie, it wasn't your
fault – in fact, if you hadn't been here when
you were I'll bet we would be in an even
worse place! But you could see how mad Big
Mike was, right? When I saw him he was
checking his watch and giving Charlie his
mad dog stare. You know he was worried as
to whether or not we'd be set up in time for
the carnival to open. A day we're not open is
a day we may not be able to pay him. Besides,
we're the biggest attraction on the midway,
and if we're *not* open – who knows? Maybe
word gets out and the whole thing doesn't

do good business. No one wants that, right? So that's when Charlie started barking orders at everyone and being all bossy (as if he knew what was supposed to be going on), trying to put on a good show for Big Mike. Once again, I keep finding someone doing something they're not supposed to because 'Charlie told me to'.

Then it happened. I'm not sure exactly where it went wrong; whether it wasn't marked right or they were just hurrying and not paying attention to what they were doing, but one of the canvas men was driving in stakes for the top when – BAM! The metal stake hits an electric cable running the genny, just underneath the dirt.

You could smell it before you even heard anything happen, you know? Electricity... Ozone... Burnt hair...

I don't think he screamed or anything. I tell you, I'm not even sure what happened, not completely. Only that there *was* yelling and running and those smells in the air.

I heard some screams, but they just sounded like some of the girls from one of the other shows. Luckily none of the townies were on the lot at that point. But I ran with the rest of them.

Big Mike was there before I got there. I don't know how he managed it. He wasn't saying anything, just wiping his forehead with the big handkerchief he carries in his overalls. It was strange to see him listening intently to Charlie, when he usually just rolls his eyes when he sees him. Then Big Mike hurried off, yelling orders to a few of the carnies, sending them out to the road to wait for the ambulance.

Charlie was on his knees next to Sam, one of our canvas men. Our performers stay the same from season to season, but canvas men tend to come and go as often as the lots. Sam was a good guy, though. A straight shooter, right? He drank a bit and kept Charlie in good company. He tended to be in the G-Top a lot, too, but he was a good guy. He was talking to Charlie, though. And Charlie was listening to him, talking back to him a bit. I went to step in closer, to find out how he was doing, but Murphy waved me back.

The ambulance arrived. It was all sirens and flashing lights, bringing attention to what had gone wrong. I was embarrassed by it. Now the other carnies would know that one of our guys was down and that it was serious. They all know how Charlie gets when he's had a few and would probably blame us if there were low crowds. And then there were crowds all around us. More people than just carnival workers standing around. Which means townies. Which means another reason for them to look down on us and hate what we do.

I don't know what happened, next. Murphy was telling me to calm down, and Charlie was asking – no, *demanding* – to know what I was going on about. And I was yelling at him about how we were now a man short and what were we going to do, when someone new broke out of the crowd and came over to the three of us, yelling at each other in the dirt.

'My name's Frank,' he said. He might have been talking to Charlie or Murphy, but he was looking at me pretty off. Maybe he couldn't figure out exactly why I was involved in this whole thing. So I jumped in quick to tell him the deal, you know?

I was like, 'What do *you* want, Townie?' before either Charlie or Murphy could say anything. This guy looks at me funny for just a moment, and then I guess he got the score because he starts talking right to me, ignoring the others.

'I may look like a townie,' he said, pretty calm-like, 'but I know the score. You're down a man. I need work.'

I gave him the once-over and then just let it fly. 'There's no room for freeloaders here. You work for us you're gonna work pretty hard.'

'Now hold on just a moment,' Murphy started in, but Charlie jumped on him pretty quick.

'You think you can run this show?' Charlie asked me, all demanding. But I didn't back down on this one, oh no! I came right back at him.

'I've been doing a fine job of it so far,' I told him. Charlie doesn't get mad or anything, but he starts kind of laughing, which scares me a little bit. Then he looks at this guy, Frank, and I can tell he doesn't like him – which just makes me want to stick it to Charlie more.

'Fine, then,' Charlie says, kinda quiet-like. 'You'll get what you got coming.' Murphy looked mad enough to eat tacks, but he just spat on the ground and the two of them walked away pretty stiffly. I turned back to this guy, Frank.

'Looks like you're hired then,' I told him, all business-like. This guy, he doesn't smile or look grateful or anything. He just reaches out his hand and we shake on it, pretty sombre. As soon as I grabbed his hand, though, there was something about him I didn't like. Can't tell you what it was specifically, greenie. Something about the way he smelled, maybe. That mix of alcohol and cigarettes that, for some reason, always makes me feel sick. But when I tell this guy what I want him to do, he gets right on to it – so I decided to let it go.

It's not until later, when the local doctor comes by to tell us that Sam will be OK in a few weeks or so, that I realise Charlie has gone – probably off drinking. Actually, I don't think we'll be seeing Sam again, greenie. Probably too close a call for him. If this guy, Frank, turns out as good as you, well... It will be just what we need!

CHAPTER 4

You know what I like, gazoonie? Sitting around before the carnival opens. You know what I mean? Just sitting around and being calm. Like we are right now. Especially when you're an early-riser like myself. It's quiet on the lot. No one else is around doing much of anything. Those feel like the best times. Almost as good as the quiet of being on the road during a jump, you know? When there is nothing to do but drive from one lot to the next.

One time, when me and Pops were on the road making a jump, we stopped at one of those little flea-trap motels he likes for me to pick out – somewhere way off the main roads. He and I watched this old film about a circus. I didn't really like it very much. There was something about a high-wire act that went wrong and a clown who was really a doctor on the run from the law... and I hated the special effects, too. They were real cheesy. Especially where the train hit the car across its tracks. Mostly I hated that they tried to make out this clown to be some kind of hero or something.

But Charlie, I guess he liked it a whole bunch. He kept sitting there and laughing to himself through the whole thing. I suppose he was laughing about the clown or something, I don't know... Everyone knows that clowns can't be heroes.

You think I'm wrong? How many clowns have *you* met? I'm not talking about the fake ones who do children's parties and that kind of nonsense. Most of them aren't the real thing – they're just forty-milers (if that) and townies who wish they were more than they are. No. All the real clowns I've ever met were some of the meanest, drunkest sons o' bitches imaginable. Just as soon throw you off the train as share a car with you. Won't let a debt go, but will happily welch on any money they owe. I, personally, am not a fan of them.

Pops, he has some funny ideas about clowns and circus folks. He's always talking about our family's history with the circus and the sideshow. He's always telling me how we're the descendants of some famous clown. Mostly, it just feels like he's talking out his... I guess I just don't get his obsession with the circus. Why would he want to be a part of that nonsense? I just think people at the circus look down on us carnies. Hardly any of them even put up a top any more! They'd rather set themselves up in an arena or some big building somewhere so they don't have to worry about it. The ones who are worth anything still put up a top – and there are only about three of them in the world, if you don't count that bunch of sissies from Canada, traipsing around in tights like a bunch of hoofers.

One time Charlie took me to see a small show – they were set up in the parking lot of an abandoned mall. They were the closest thing I've ever seen to a circus being with it. They had a single ring, lots of animals, high-wire acts and some dangerous stunts… and they dinged the rubes between every act! About halfway through, I went to get some popcorn at the concession stand – and I'll tell you what – the girl who sold it to me had just been up in the rigging doing a trapeze act a few minutes before. *That* is what I am talking about! Someone who is with it, who works hard and understands the life we have.

Me? I like my life here with the carnival, running this show – well, helping Charlie manage it. I don't know what he'd do without me at all. But bringing in you and this guy Frank, plus having Murphy and our performers, that's going to make a difference, I think. I hope.

Murphy and me, we used to have lots of talks about the show and what kinds of things we could do. Especially back when Charlie was teaching me stunts and things to do for the shows he was planning – now, those were the days! Anyways, Murphy spent a lot of time talking to me and Charlie about what the old shows used to do – and let me tell you, gazoonie, they did some amazing things! Of course, back in the day, they used to do a lot more than we do now. I mean, Murphy was telling me some of the big shows had fifty people or more there to work the whole thing. There were canvas men whose only job was to make sure the top got up, and guys to work the lights and sound – and that's before you even added the performers, stage managers and other stuff. Can you imagine?

Murphy told me that some of the shows, well they used to be reviews, off the big stages from London and New York, and that they'd package them up into something that could travel more easily. Sometimes I think about what it would have been like to be running a show back then. From what Murphy tells me, they would even supply you with everything you needed if you brought them a show: a top, banner line, all the lights and sound – everything! You'd just bring the performers and acts, maybe some of the crew and such – and they'd pay you out proper *and* you could take whatever you could get from the inside. No one made you account for any of it. That's what I dream about sometimes. How I'd bring in Delilah to help me out, and I'd get me my *own* show – and Charlie could go off and do whatever he wants.

No. No, I haven't really talked to her since we got here. OK – I haven't talked to her at all. But, sure she's my girl! I told you, didn't I? She just has some other things on her mind is all. What with her momma passing away during the off-season... and I don't think her family's show is doing that well either. Now, you didn't hear it from me, but some of the other carnies have been telling me to stay away from her – just to leave her alone. I imagine it's that, with her momma's passing and their show having problems, they figure that I'm just hassling her or something. Doesn't surprise me, none, I'll tell you that. In a way it pleases me. See, we look out for each other on the lot.

A single-o is a show that just has one attraction. One thing that you're paying to see, and it's usually something pretty stationary. You're not seeing a show like that with us. There's no bally out front or anything, except maybe a grind tape that lures you up to the monkey box to pay your money to get in. Then you walk in, take a look at it, and walk back out. Pretty simple, huh? Thing is, for a single-o to really make money and attract a crowd, it has to be something live. You can't use bouncers or gaffs (I'll tell you a bit more about them in a minute) – not even pickled punks, because that stuff won't keep a mark's attention. Pickled punks are what we call deformed babies in jars – they used to be pretty common until the do-gooders made it too tough to put them on display. After laws about displaying real babies went into effect in lots of places, most of the showmen started making babies out of plaster and rubber (which is why they're called bouncers) and using those, instead. Thing is gaffs like that often look better than the real thing! Gaffs are anything fake – but for most showmen that means they faked something using taxidermy, or sometimes a bigger trick. No, for a single-o, it has to be something alive, like a live 'mermaid' in a pool or headless woman trick. Sure, those might still be a gaff in a way – but they're more of an illusion – *and* you have to have someone alive there to really make it work under the top. It's that or, even better, a real mutant animal like Delilah's family's show. They have a six-legged cow!

Yeah, yeah – I know. But it's true! I've seen her (the cow, I mean). She's real, all right, but dumb. I suppose all cows are dumb – but this one is really stupid. It's a great show, though. It really brings the crowds in, especially in the cities (I guess the farmers feel they see enough of that kind of thing), but... it's a cow. It has to be taken care of. It needs food and water and to be walked. You have to clean up after animals. That's why Charlie won't have anything to do with any kind of live animal show. Can't say I blame him – I don't want to clean up after animals either.

That and the fact that every time some do-gooder gets it in their head the carnies are abusing their animals, seems like everyone comes running in to try to shut the whole show down. If only they knew – these animals get treated better than most of the people working here!

Anyway, I tried to get a few moments alone with Delilah before the last jump, but it didn't happen. Then I keep wandering by her joint to get her attention, but she hasn't seen me yet. Probably because her dad's been keeping an eye on everything she's been up to lately. Don't know why. Maybe he thinks she's not doing her job and that's why the numbers are low for their show. Maybe if he worked the ticket box a bit more and didn't spend so much time worrying about what she's doing, it would be OK.

Delilah's family has had a show on this circuit for a couple of seasons. What I'm telling you is, this ain't no seasonal fling, son! Why, Delilah and I used to be pretty tight before her dad put her to work on their show this time around. Guess he didn't feel she was really old enough for the responsibility of taking the money before. Now, I've noticed that their show has gotten a few more chumps hanging around it since she came to sit in the chair. Her momma used to, you know… sit in the chair and take tickets, I mean, but she passed on sometime between the end of last season and the beginning of this one. I guess that's the other reason her dad is keeping her close at hand, too.

I don't know what they do in the off-season – and I'm not sure what happened to her momma, either. I guess I keep hoping she'll tell me about it.

After a bit, I'll shove on over there and see if I can't get her attention. Before I do that, though, I need to do my walk-through of the top and make sure everything is OK. Not that I think anything is wrong, mind you, I'm sure everyone did exactly what they were supposed to do. But, when someone new, like Frank, is on the payroll, I like to keep a close eye on what he's doing. Especially after Sam's accident.

But he sure seems to know his stuff, does Frank. He didn't waste any time getting the top up and the banner line going. It's almost like he's done it before – like he's 'with it', you know? I guess it doesn't matter because the bigger thing is that as soon as Frank was on deck, Charlie was nowhere to be found.

Sure, I heard some grumbling from some of the others, especially Murphy – but I'm not too worried about it. Honestly, I'm more worried about trying to get some time with Delilah. So, if this guy Frank can help to make sure things get done the way they are supposed to pretty quickly – and I can get some time with my girl – that's what I'm going to do.

CHAPTER 5

You've seen me on the stage, gazoonie – I don't worry about anything, do I? I can do a big escape stunt, then lay on a bed of nails, and still chat up all the girlies, too. Like I told you, they don't call me the 'Clown Prince of Sideshow' for nothing, you know! I don't worry about my own safety, right? Why should I worry about anything else? Honestly?

I don't like to think of myself as someone who worries. Worrying about things doesn't do any good. Especially if you can't do anything about whatever it is that's wrong. It just uses up energy that could be turned to something else. Something more productive, maybe.

Sometimes, though, things start to get to me. Not big things, mind you... just the little ones. Like today, for instance...

After the shows the other night, I slept in a bit, right? Just like most of you do, too. That's why Charlie says that the carnival is the greatest job in the world for lazy people – we get to sleep in all the time. I mean you and I know that isn't always true – there are plenty of days we never get to sleep at all! Anyways, my thought was that I'd have a little walk around the lot first thing this morning – especially if it took me over by Delilah's family camp on the back yard. But I don't want to look like I'm trying to get her to talk to me, right? I mean – I can't let the carnies think that I am *looking* for her to talk to me. After all, I am the 'Clown Prince of Sideshow', aren't I?

Anyway, today, after I got up, I got it into my head that I was going to take a walk around the lot, making sure to take some time in the back yard. Remember what I told you? The back yard is a carny's home;

it's the living lot, where almost everyone stays. Doesn't matter if they're in a tent, or a trailer, or sharing a space in a bunkhouse; it sure beats carrying the banner, which is sleeping in the top because you have no place else to go. And since it *is* their home, that means I was going to have to walk careful. I mean you had a home once, right greenie? Sure, now you're in a bunkhouse – but you look like maybe you had some folks who actually had a house they lived in. And back then, you wouldn't let just anyone go walking through your kitchen, would you? It's the same thing.

But you never can tell. Sometimes the whole back yard is open to any and everyone, it seems. I don't know why carnies would suddenly become all hospitable – unless there was something in it for them. Usually, everyone is a lot more open to having guests and meeting up at the beginning of the season, so they can figure out who is who and what is what. Meetings like that are what set the tone for the rest of the season, gazoonie, if you know what I mean.

But later on during the run everyone wants a little more privacy. Day in and day out of being together on the road and in the lot starts putting everyone on edge. Then a beef or three might start up, and before you know it areas of the back yard just ain't so friendly any more. Still, when you're as with it as I am, it shouldn't matter too much where your feet decide to take you as long as you can BC.

So, I set my feet towards taking me for a walk around the lot. I'm doing it nice and easy, taking my time – not making a beeline for her dad's trailer or anything like that – when I look over and what do I see but a couple of the more familiar faces.

Like I told you, everyone on the lot knows me, so I can go just about anywhere just about any time with no problem. So when I saw Mutt and Jeff, I just told them Al-A-Ga-Zam (remember – the way to say 'hello' to the agents that I told you?), figuring they were on their way to the cook shack from their beds, and went on my way. And next thing I know, they're standing in my way, wanting to chat.

'Hey there, Tony,' said Mutt. 'What are you doing?' Jeff just nodded – he tends not to talk much.

'Just on a little walkabout,' I replied, nonchalant-like. 'Seeing the sights. You know.'

'We was just talking as we was heading over to the cook shack,' Mutt continued, his tongue licking over the couple of teeth which appears to be all he has left, 'and we was thinking you might be able to help us out.'

Now, normally I'm quick to help anyone out who comes to me for information. Today, though, I have a mission on my mind and don't want to get distracted by anything else. I went to step around the two of them with a quick, 'Sorry. Busy.' But before I got too far, Jeff was right in front of me, and Mutt's hand was on my arm.

'No, no,' Mutt said to me. 'We won't take no for an answer!'

His hand on my arm was pretty friendly-like, but I could feel his strength behind it. And Jeff didn't have a tent stake in his hand, but he definitely seemed intent on keeping me from going my own way.

Look, greenie, I'm not saying I was afraid. I mean, you know me, I'm not afraid of anyone or anything. But these guys are carnies of the old school through and through – and I knew that if I gave them too much trouble, they might just take a poke at me just to show me who's boss. So I let myself be led off, with the two of them glancing over their shoulders several times, as we headed in the direction of the cook shack.

Did they have questions for me? Yeah, I suppose... I mean, they bought me some coffee and picked my brain about turning a tip, my escape stunts and... hmmm. I guess a little bit about this new guy Frank, who's on the payroll now. I guess, thinking about it, I don't know if they were trying to keep me from something in the back yard, or if they really wanted to know about this guy.

So, while I was mad at having been pulled away from seeing Delilah, it led me to something else.

Remember how I told you Charlie hasn't been around much since Frank has been working the top? Well, you can imagine my surprise when I finally pulled myself away from the cook shack and headed back to our joint. As I was walking up, I could hear voices talking inside – not real loud, mind you – but raised up like they were trying to keep it quiet so no one could overhear, even though they were mad. So I snuck up to the laces, you know, around the edge where the sides of the top lace up together, and stuck my ear up to it to listen in.

It was Charlie and Frank having a beef. And, I mean, really getting into it. I don't know what started the whole thing, but by the time I got up to it, this is what I heard:

First thing I hear Charlie say is, 'Just who do you think you are? No one is going to go for that!'

Then Frank came back with, 'Oh, I think they will. If you didn't think so, then they'd all know, wouldn't they?'

'Doesn't matter what they know,' Charlie told him. 'Or what someone thinks they know.'

Frank started to answer, 'Yeah, you can say...'

But Charlie interrupted him, saying, 'Things are a lot different now than they used to be. And don't you think for a moment that I'm going to let you say a damn thing to Tony! You just stay away from him! He knows all he needs to know.'

And Frank, he said, 'That boy don't know much of anything, does he? Or you would've spoke up when you saw me on the lot that day. But you'd had a few, hadn't you Charlie? Yeah, you had all right. I've seen it before and I know just what happens when you do that, don't I?'

I couldn't see the look on my pops' face

at that point; but I had a pretty good idea what his face looked like right then. Like a bad dog caught piddling on the rug or something. I've seen him with that look plenty of times. I closed my eyes, trying to picture the inside of the top, imagining the two of them facing off on the little stage.

Now Charlie ain't no slouch, mind you – but the years of *running* the show rather than setting it up have left him a little soft. My pops stood a good few inches taller than this guy, Frank. But Frank carries himself in that wiry kind of way that only a carny in his prime seems to have. Tight, corded muscles used to lifting rope, his arms ending in the big worn and beaten hands that come from heaving the big pipes, stakes and sledgehammers. A dark look on his permanently sunburned face makes his bright blue eyes burn with an empty flame. Broken nose. A few tattoos. Just looking at Frank made me think of what someone who spent his whole life with bar fights and hard living should look like. Next to him, Charlie looks kind of like a desk-jockeying marshmallow.

I was surprised then that I could hear Charlie muttering something to Frank under his breath then... something dark, mean and ugly. I don't know what he was saying, but the hair on the back of my neck stood up just to hear the sounds coming from him. Never, ever have I heard my pops talk to anyone like that. Not even at his angriest.

And I guess Frank wasn't used to being talked to like that either, because by the time I heard Frank answer, his voice wasn't filled with the bravado it had had before. There was something else in it. Fear? Maybe. Respect? Definitely. I heard him answer my pops, saying, 'I'll do what I promised you I would. You keep up your end of our bargain, and I'll keep up mine.'

They may have said more, but I snuck away then.

I don't know what they were talking about, either, greenie. It just made me think that maybe there's more to this guy Frank than I'd thought. Will you keep an eye on him, for me? I mean, I would do it, but I still have something I need to do.

Well, sure, I'm still going to go over to see Delilah! But I'll do it tonight, after the show. Didn't forget that we're doing the grind, did you? There are marks who are begging to be separated from their money, son! But I'll meet back up with you later.

Psst! Greenie!! Yeah, you. Over here!

Get down. Down! Look, just keep it quiet for a moment, all right? Staying behind this trailer may not be the most comfortable thing in the world, but it's what we're going to do for the moment.

What happened? How do you know anything happened?

OK, OK. Yes. Something happened. But keep your trap shut and I'll tell you about it. Quietly... OK?

I did what I told you I was going to do. I took a walk over to Delilah's trailer. This time, I thought I'd avoid getting stopped by anyone, by reading the midway while I walked along. You know, 'read the midway' – I walked with my head down, looking for change and anything else the chumps might have dropped on their way out of the carnival.

But when I got near the entrance to the back yard, what do you think I see? Mutt and Jeff, who were hanging around the gate. Almost like they were waiting for me. I kept an eye on them though, as soon as I saw them, because I had no desire to get distracted again. So I kept my head down and headed around through the back way.

So I figured, as I'm used to heights and climbing and things, that I'd scale over the fence using the Light Plant – that's the big truck with the generators on it – to get myself through. Now, it probably meant that I would have to walk back *out* of the gate past Mutt and Jeff, but I figured I'd be OK at that point.

It was easy enough to get over to where I wanted to go – to Delilah's trailer. But when I got there, gazoonie... Well, when I got there, not all of the lights were off. So I was listening outside quietly, beneath the lit-up window that used to be her window – just to make sure it was still hers right? I hear voices – not just her voice, right? But a couple of voices – and it sounds like her and her father talking really quickly and urgently. Then I feel the whole trailer shift – like someone threw themselves into the side of it. And then more noises from inside. It was like things were being thrown around. Like someone was getting slapped or hit. I could hear loud voices, but couldn't tell what they were saying. And then it sounded like crying.

I froze. I completely froze. I didn't know what to do. Should I get help? Or try to get in?

Just then, I heard a yell behind me. I turned around and saw what looked like Mutt or Jeff – one of the carnies, anyway, it wasn't a townie – running towards me and yelling. Well, a noise like that would wake up the whole lot, and... Well I just ran, greenie. I ran as quick as I could, not paying attention to where I was going.

Within a few moments I'd put some good distance between me and Delilah's trailer, and I started thinking I should turn around and tell whoever it was chasing me, who it was they were after. I mean, maybe they thought I was just some townie pervert sneaking around the trailers, being a peeping tom or something. I know I shouldn't have run – but I did.

When I turned around, though, there wasn't anybody there. I guess I'd lost them as I ran through the lot. I was hoping that whoever it was who'd chased me off had heard what was going on in Delilah's trailer, and maybe put a stop to it. But, if I went back to check, I'd have to answer why I was out there, right? That's what made me stop and think. That's what made me head back here instead of going back.

What would you have done?

CHAPTER 6

Who's that? Is that you, greenie?

Yeah, you can come in. Sorry about the mess, but being stuck here in the trailer is not the best way to keep a clean house. Thanks! A good cup of joe was just what I needed. Nothing like a good cup of coffee to give you a quick lift. Heck, even a bad cup of joe would be better than drinking nothing but juice, like I have been. Stupid doctors.

Well sure I'm healing up all right; but take a look at this, would you? I'm going to be limping around for a while with this stupid... Ah, I just can't believe that it all went so badly wrong so quickly.

Sure, sure. I'll tell you exactly what happened. Sit down over there. Just shove that stuff off that chair. So our night was going along like any other, right? I mean, we've had a few blue dates in a row, so it was time to finally bring in some cash, right? Sometimes these carnival rules that Big Mike has to go along with – Dollar Days and other stupid ideas – I mean, who thinks up these things?

You know what I mean by Dollar Days, gazoonie. Don't get that look on your face like you haven't put in even a single day on the midway. That's when whoever it is running the lot, the one who called in Big Mike to bring the carnival there, decides to run some special on the rides and attractions. What was it this last time? One ticket for each ride or something dumb… Other times they offer wristbands to all the kiddies for a huge discount so they can ride all the rides – or make it so everyone rides on kids' tickets. Always something dumb.

Now, when they do it to the ride jocks – well honestly, why should we care? But the thing is, sometimes they'll try to arrange it so the special includes the shows, too. Now a single-o, like the six-legged cow Delilah's daddy has, is one thing. But, for them to do it to us? It's ridiculous! Our nut is huge compared to most of the jocks here. We have a full staff to pay, plus the space rental, the parking for our trucks and trailers, hooking up to the genny... When they include *our* show, we're just messed up, aren't we? We can't ever make that money up unless management decides to just burn the lot.

You know how I've told you that Big Mike don't put up with any of us ripping off the townies or doing anything bad to anyone else? We never pull a red light job, where we get people to work for us then drive off without paying them, or burn anyone – but after a few days of this mess, I think even he's changing his tune! Yeah, he's definitely not interested in coming back to this locale at all. That's what it means to 'burn the lot'. I'm talking about going ahead and letting the agents just take everybody's money and not care if we or any other carnival is ever allowed to come back to this town again.

Wouldn't bother me none to never come back here again, let me tell you!

So, anyway, we haven't been making our nut. That's the amount of money we need to bring in to cover our expenses. I know it, Charlie knows it, and most of the show and crew do, too. I bet even you can see it, can't you? After the past few days of being ripped off by the lot, it was finally our time to pull out all the stops and make some cash. Now, for a showman like myself, the best way to bring in the crowds is to put on the best show I can. Word starts building throughout the lot when a show's really good, then those townies take it back to their friends, and next thing you know, the place is full of people ready to see what's going on.

Yeah, I know some of the nonsense that the other shows have been telling you. How it's our job to rip off the rubes without any thought to them. How does that phrase go? 'Never give a sucker an even break, or wisen up a chump,' that's what Charlie told me some of the agents always say. But Charlie doesn't buy into that and, more importantly, neither does Big Mike. And you don't want to either, greenie. Trust me on that!

So, it was finally our night. I'd been doing the counts; I knew we needed to make our nut, and that we needed to make it quick! And I figured the way to do it was to put something up on the bally that was way bigger than anyone else was doing. I worked it out with the rest of the troupe, we would push the grind as much as possible. See, we all know that Charlie, when he's the outside talker, doesn't always like to push to turn the tip... And when he's like that, Murphy, who's on the inside as the lecturer – well he's not in a big hurry to push the show. But the faster we do the shows, the more we can do in a night – and the more customers we can get to pay to come in!

The plan was to get Charlie distracted into doing other things at various times throughout the night, so that I could take over as the outside talker and really work on turning the tips. I figured the faster I turned the tips, the faster Murphy would work the acts inside. We (all the performers) also all agreed that we would keep our acts short, so it would help in speeding things through. Heck, even the half-and-half said she could make the blow-off go over in a really big way!

So we launched into the night. As always when we opened, the midway was slow. We took our time, conserving our energies, getting ready to launch my plan, right? The sun was still up as we began, just like always, and the crowds stayed away. But come dark, I'm on the bally doing a little fire-eating and I can see the bigger crowds start flowing down the midway towards us. I give the signal to Jerry – he's the show's cowboy – and he comes out of the top to pull Charlie aside about a problem with the half-and-half act. Jerry makes it out to be big enough so that Charlie gives me the nod to take over talking the bally, then he heads around to the back of the top.

Thing is, we all know that if Charlie has to step away from the bally, he probably won't be back for a while. I may not like it, but I know my pops. A moment away is a moment to get a snort. As if some alcohol will really make him a better talker – or whatever he thinks he's doing.

As soon as Charlie is gone, I really start laying it on the townies. You know the drill – about how they'll be amazed by the wonders inside our joint. First, I start off with a couple big bursts of fire. Fire always helps gather a crowd. Having *you* as a shill, just stopping dead in the middle of the midway so it causes a jam of people right then, doesn't hurt, either. And as the crowds slow down I start in with my crack – that's the words that are going to bring this mob into a tip, ready to be turned into an audience in our joint.

'My friends,' I start saying, nice and friendly-like, 'you are just in time. Just in time for the big show. Come closer, come closer. That's the big, free show that we are about to perform for you, right on this stage, right now. What I'm going to do right now is bring out our performers. That's right, friends. All of them are making their way out to the stage right now just to perform for you. That's right, a free show, right here, right now.' Then I lean back like I'm yelling into the tent, 'Come on, now. Bring everyone out. The sword-swallower, the fire-eater. That's right, all of them!' Then I turn back to the audience, saying, 'Move in closer, move in closer. We are going to do this show, we are going to do it for free, and I do *not* want you to miss a moment of it!'

So the crowd is gathering closer and closer now, expecting a free show. I've given a nod and a wink to a couple of the girls (and a couple older ladies, too), so they're dragging their men in with them, creating an even bigger traffic jam in front of the bally stage. All that is making people stop, who probably wouldn't have done so otherwise.

'You may have seen some bursts of flame,' I go on, 'but that is nothing compared to how hot it will get inside. You see this girl?' I ask them, pointing out Bettie the contortionist, who gives a little twist. After all, *I* might be able to interest the ladies, but I need to give the guys a reason to want to come into the show! 'Well she can do things so amazing, that the sheriff made us bring in a doctor to verify she wouldn't be hurt while on our stage. He doesn't know how she does it – he just knows that she can! And take a look at this gentleman making his way to the stage right now!' I point out Travis to them, continuing, 'Some people will tell you it's the normal ones you have to look out for – come in closer, friends; we need to make some room in the back there – and this young man is no exception. Take a look at his particular skill: the ability to swallow twenty-six inches of solid steel and remain unhurt!' And while Travis swallows the sword, I continue, 'Now you may think this is something, but it's nothing compared with what he'll do on the inside folks. Trust me. This young man – well a neon tube and a sense of daring will make him do the unthinkable. You will *see* the light all the way down to his insides! Buy your ticket now!'

Of course, greenie, you know that's your cue to go to the monkey box – the ticket booth – and act like you're buying a ticket. There always has to be someone who starts the rush! Of course, you've been there nights when I'm so on that there are rubes lining up long before you get the chance to kick it off... But it never hurts for you to be there for the moment things start to slow down. Charlie, when he does it, he likes to offer discounts like, 'everyone for a child's ticket' kind of stuff. I hate that. I think if we do it right, then we don't need to do that stuff.

So once the chumps make it under the top, they see all the acts, right? Wait a minute! You've never seen the show, have you, gazoonie? We always have you so busy running around you never get to! Well, it goes like this:

First, Murphy rolls a box into the centre of the pit and starts his talking, while Bettie unfolds herself out of it. Then she rolls the box back off just in time for Jerry, all dressed up like a cowboy, to come in and crack his whip a few times. That always makes people jump! Then, usually, we're at a point where I can leave the bally and do a straightjacket escape or something. As soon as that is done, I head out to start the next bally and Abdul comes on with his fakir stunts. He might stick skewers through his biceps or chin – all without bleeding. Or he might swallow a piece of string, then cut into his own belly and pull the string out! Murphy usually does a quick magic trick before bringing out the blade box for Bettie. Yeah, you know all about that one, don't you?

After that, Jerry does some knife-throwing, using Sharon as his target girl, then Travis does his full sword-swallowing act. After that we're in the push to get in the last three acts, so depending on the bally, either me, Travis or Abdul does the bed of nails, then there's another act before hitting the fire-breathing finale. And, of course, while the audience is recovering from that, Murphy launches into the crack to send them over the edge to see the blow-off – our half-and-half.

So that's ten acts in about thirty minutes. When not on stage, the performers are on the bally stage building the tip to turn into the joint. Of course, the audience can come in whenever they want, and leave whenever they want – but between the push for the blade box and the blow-off, we expect that they'll leave when they start seeing the same acts over again. That's why there are no seats or anything in the top. We don't want them to get comfortable – we want them to pay to get in, ding them while they're inside, then get them back out from under the canvas so someone *else* can pay to get in.

Like clockwork, right? I mean, you've seen us work, haven't you, greenie? Like a well-oiled machine practically... So what happened to me? Well – as near as I can figure – it was something like this:

Since Jerry had dragged Charlie off, I'd been turning the tip pretty regular-like. They were coming in fast enough that Murphy and everyone seemed on their top game. I mean, they didn't all seem too happy, but I figured it was because I was really making them work for a change. Anyway, just as I suspected, Charlie was really slow in coming back from our 'emergency'. Who knows – maybe something really was wrong with the blow-off.

We'd done maybe two or three full shows when it happened. Don't tell anyone, gilly, but I was not as on top of things as I should've been. Guess I was worried about Delilah. Not paying attention to what you're doing, especially when it's as dangerous as what I do, can get you hurt.

Anyways, to make a long story even longer, it was the third or fourth show, and I'm all wound up to do the huge fire act. I might do a couple of small bursts on the bally stage, but on the inside I really let it go with my 'fountain of flame' act. See, what I do is fill my mouth full of the fuel, and then, using two torches, I start spitting it out in a fine mist. Once that mist catches fire from the lit torches, I pull them away – letting the fuel continue to catch fire as I spit it out until it's all gone.

It's a risky act, and Charlie doesn't like me doing it. Never mind that he is the one who taught me how to do it! But part of our deal with me doing it is that he is the one to pre-measure all the fuel out for the bursts. Too much fuel means too much flame. It could catch the top on fire or worse, some dumb townie could light up! That would be really bad. So Charlie tends to be really careful with it.

Of course, I know my da and what he tends to do, so I usually double-check everything. I thought I had, too, but I guess I was distracted – like I told you.

As soon as I put the fuel in my mouth, I knew I was in trouble. There was too much, and it didn't taste right. Like it was a weird mix of gasoline, kerosene and who knows what else, all dumped in there together. I guess I should have spit it out right then, but it was the high point of the show, and I just wanted to – I don't know – get back out on the bally, I guess. Turn the next tip. See if I could see Delilah from the bally stage… It doesn't matter now, I guess.

As I started to spit, the fuel caught, way too quickly, burning its way up the stream to my face! I turned my face and moved the torches away, but it was too late. I felt the flame licking over my face. I smelled burning hair. And I guess I panicked a bit too, because I don't remember much else except struggling to get the fire off me.

Trying to get the fuel out of my mouth, I guess I must have spit it out onto my clothes, because my pants leg caught fire as well. Luckily, I knew enough to keep my eyes closed, and to drop to the ground and roll around. Good thing this wasn't the wooden stage we use sometimes! Since we set up this top with a pit, there was a coating of sand on the ground, and that helped.

All I heard was yelling and people running around. I guess it was the crowd leaving while the performers gathered around me. Murphy was the first one to get to me, and then I could hear Charlie next to me. He was yelling orders to other people and calling to me. He sounded almost crazy. Can you believe that? My own pops yelling at me for catching on fire?

It took a while for things to calm down enough. Charlie still hasn't really talked to me since then. Murphy told me Big Mike sprung for the fancy doctor they sent in. Thank goodness they didn't send an ambulance or anything. Murphy also told me to take it easy for a few days. But he wouldn't say anything else. None of the people from the show have come to talk to me but you, greenie. Guess they're all pretty sore that I messed up.

But I'll be back. You'll see.

CHAPTER 7

So you found me, eh?

Well, you're here. Might as well sit down and make yourself comfortable. On top of the Light Plant isn't the most comfortable place to be hiding – but it sure beats hiding under one of the rigs. That's the thing about carnies – most of them never look up.

But you knew where to find me, didn't you, gilly? Maybe you're not such a gazoonie after all...

No, no. I'll come down in a bit. 'Turn myself in', or whatever it is they want to call it. I know most of the lot doesn't know why I did what I did. But you do, don't you, greenie? Do me a favour though, will you? Don't tell anyone. I won't have anyone thinking less of Delilah, or looking at me with any kind of sympathy, like they would some punk. It's bad enough I end up hobbling around this lot the past week. Can't do a show. Can't bring in any money. Doctor coming around and bothering me when all I really need to do is get back on the boards.

No – I did what I had to do, and I'm not sorry for it. Not even a little bit.

Ever since the accident it just hasn't been that easy. You know, Murphy has been taking care of me quite a bit. Charlie hasn't done much more than stick his head in my bunk every once in a while to look at me. He's hardly even said much more than to ask how I was doing. I can hear him and Murphy talking quietly in the main room of the trailer sometimes. Then I hear him leaving, and Murphy sticks in his head to say, 'Hey, kid. How you holding up?'

One night – pretty late, because there wasn't a peep from the shows or carnival – I heard something in my room. Guess I wasn't too fast asleep or anything, because I didn't jump up. Just opened my eyes a little bit to peek through and see what it was. Charlie was in my room, leaning against the doorway from our trailer's main room. He didn't say anything, or try to wake me up. I just lay there looking at him for – oh, I don't know... it seemed like forever. I started wondering if he was wishing I wasn't along on this show.

Then I watched him take a deep draw from the bottle he had in his hand, before he turned around and shuffled out. Quiet as death he was, coming in and out of my room in the pitch black. I was lying there kind of scared, wondering what he might do – and thinking about how many times he might have snuck into my room to stand and watch me with that look on his face.

It's been years since Charlie laid a hand on me – did you know that, greenie? It was one of the first times he started on the bottle, right after I lost my mum. He went on a tear – there seemed to be empty bottles and cans as far as the eye could see – and he was throwing things, yelling, cursing. I was pretty scared at the time. I had run up to him to try to put the brakes on him and he just... Well, I'm not really sure what happened after that, actually. He sort of grabbed, twisted and threw me all at the same time. We were on a cart or something high up, and I went flying off it onto the ground. I don't remember much after that, but suddenly Murphy had me in his arms, and my da, he was yelling and crying and trying to get to me. But Murphy wouldn't let him.

I haven't thought about it in a while. Almost like I can't remember it – but that's what happened. I don't remember seeing Charlie drink much after that. I mean – I know that he does it. Drink, I mean. Everyone knows that Charlie drinks as much as he can. But since that day he seems to go to a lot more trouble to hide what he is doing.

That's why I was scared watching him that night. I haven't actually seen him take a snort from a bottle in years. If he's been doing that, will he come after me, again? Especially if he's angry with me or doesn't want me around.

It's those thoughts that I hate, greenie. I'm not one to worry, I told you before – but thoughts like that have a tendency to nag at you, not letting you go about your day like you should. Between the thought that Charlie might want to get rid of me, and worrying about Delilah, I haven't felt quite right.

So then I'm out reading the midway a bit later in the afternoon, looking for stray stuff on the ground, and Murphy falls into step beside me. I ignore him for as long as I can, but then he starts talking to me.

'How you doing there, kid?' he asks, all nonchalant. 'Getting some exercise?'

'Don't be dumb,' I said to him. 'I'm a carny. Exercising is for suckers with too much time on their hands. I work for a living.'

'So, you're looking for anything the chumps may have left behind.' He laughed a bit. 'Just like I taught you, kid. Remember that?'

Of course I do, but I can't really tell him that, can I? Murphy is the only person I've ever let call me kid. Not even Charlie gets to do that. But I'm being tough, right? I need to harden myself up for what he's going to say, so I just keep on walking. And he keeps right up with me.

'Look, kid,' he starts in, again, 'I need to talk to you about the show.'

'Talk to Charlie,' I tell him, 'he's the one in charge, isn't he?'

Murphy stops me, forcing me to look up at him. And when I look into his eyes, I see real concern there. I never expected that.

'Tony,' Murphy said, 'as much as I want you to be, you're not just some punk kid. You've seen the receipts. You know the take. You know what our nut is.' He stopped a moment, glancing up and down the lot. Then kind of motioned for us to keep moving, like he didn't want us standing still. And this is the first time I can think of that he's called me by my name. Must be something big – so I go with him.

'The show isn't doing well,' Murphy says, flat out. 'Big Mike has always done right by us – maybe even when he shouldn't have – but even he can't overlook how often the show's been late getting to a lot. We keep losing the prime spots, which means our take isn't as good as it used to be. The working acts are good – but the rubes aren't as interested in them these days. Then we lose Sam. Then we almost lose you.

'Now I know that wasn't your fault,' he said, motioning me to calm down before I can get a word out. Guess he knows the score about how I feel. 'Everyone knows it. But it's something of a jinx, isn't it? We all depend on you, Tony, you know that. And now this guy Frank is starting to get everyone riled up, isn't he?'

'What do you mean?' I asked him. I haven't thought about Frank much, but suddenly I remember the conversation I overheard him and Charlie having. But I don't tell Murphy about it. Not now. I can hear anger in Murphy's voice as he continues.

'That guy ain't no townie, kid. And he knows more than a thing or two about this show. He knows the crowds ain't what they're supposed to be, and he knows we're struggling to get everyone paid. And he's telling the others.'

'He can say whatever he wants to the rest of the show,' I told him. 'They know us. They know we'll come through. We've never let them down.'

Murphy shrugged, 'He's not just saying it to the people in our show, kid. He's been saying it all over the lot. That starts rumours. Rumours tend to spread in a place like this. And after a while rumours start to take on a ring of truth. And that ring of truth gets back to management. And when

Big Mike gets a real wind of what's going around, he's going to act on it.'

I was mad now. 'Why would anyone believe what *he* says? Why should they listen to anything from him? They *know* us!'

'That's the thing, kid,' Murphy looked at me, hard. 'They know him, too. And they believe him, because some of what he is saying is true. The show really is in trouble!'

'We'll pull it out,' I told him, but he wasn't going for it.

'We can pull it out or not,' he said to me. 'But this guy is also saying other stuff. When told with the truth, even false things can *seem* real. And that is all it takes to make people believe *everything* he says. Once they start doing that, the show can fall apart.'

Murphy stopped a moment. We were in a quiet part of the lot. The sun was beating down on us and the dust was scratching the back of my throat.

'What do you want me to do?' I asked Murphy, meeting his eyes.

Murphy looked away from me again, staring off at the horizon like he was thinking. But I knew he didn't really have an answer. He had something else on his mind.

'I want you to think long and hard about what I said,' Murphy told me. 'I want you to consider it with what's coming. You never wanted to be a kid, Tony. And now, there's no turning back. You're an adult. You have responsibility for what's going to happen. Man to man, I am telling you this. I want you to be ready.'

He looked at me pretty sombre-like, then reached out and shook my hand. That's when I knew he was serious. About everything.

Murphy walked off then, not reading the midway any more, but with his head high and his eyes toward the horizon, like he was watching for an upcoming storm. Me? I didn't know what to do really. I continued to walk around the lot, thinking about what Murphy had told me, and what I'd seen and heard.

Anyway, after wandering around for a while, I looked up and found myself near Delilah's joint. You know, where the six-legged cow is. I didn't plan it or anything, I just happened to find myself there. So I forced myself to walk right up to it.

Of *course* I was hoping she would be there, greenie! I've been thinking about what I'd heard when I sat beneath the window of her trailer ever since it happened. I practically can't think of anything else. And, as I was thinking about what Murphy had said to me, I realised that if I was going to be a man, then I needed to tell her what I thought. I just had it in my head that if I could talk to her – let her know that I knew what was going on, I mean – she might come with me. I could protect her from whoever it was tossing her around. By which I mean her father, right?

But as I walked up to their tent, I heard something. Maybe I should have walked away right then. Gone to get someone else. Found Murphy, maybe. I should have done anything but walk into that top. Because right on the inside, huddled against the stall where they keep the cow, Delilah was crying. And not just crying, she was bawling, and she looked beaten up, I guess. I was just... well, shocked, greenie. So that I didn't know what to do for a moment.

All I could do was listen to her sobbing. Watch her shaking as she held on to the bars of that stupid cow's stall while tears ran down her cheeks. It's crazy the things you remember when a moment like that hits you. I'll never forget the look on her face when she saw me. She tried to pull her jacket up over her arms and shoulders – I guess to cover up the bruises.

I was only there for a moment, but in that moment something cracked. I mean, something broke inside me, right then. All I could think about was that I hadn't said anything that night at her trailer; that I'd run, instead, you know?

So as soon as I saw her, I ran again. Only this time, I ran right for the cook shack.

Oh, yeah, I didn't stop for anything, son. I ran as fast as I could right to where I knew her father would be. I was pretty sure I'd got the whole picture. I was going to make sure he never put his hands on her again.

I didn't slow down until I got there. Normally I'd go in careful, because everyone is there. The cook shack is the main place for everyone to socialise whenever they can, talk about the next jump, the red dates or the blue ones. It's usually a safe place, off-limits for any beefs, you know. But whatever – I was out for his blood.

I thought that when I went for him it would be something like in one of those old westerns I used to watch with Charlie, back when we had stopovers at the hotels. I would walk in the door, and then people would clear-off when I told him to come outside with me. Then once I had him outside I'd work him over a bit. He'd surrender to me because I'm the good guy, and he's the bad guy. But, it didn't work out that way.

Don't know what it was. There must have been some look on my face, because as soon as I walked in the place, I saw some people scramble for the door. Then almost right off I saw him, standing near where the coffee is. That's when I snapped.

A kind of red haze settled over my eyes, and the next thing I know I'm jumping over the table between me and him, tackling him to the ground. I guess calm and cool went out the window, huh? So I get him to the ground and I'm just swinging on him with all I got. I don't know. There are fights like you see in the movies, then there's the real thing. I've even seen a few real scraps. A clem or two. But it's different to be in the middle of one.

I guess I was just thinking that right was on my side – and I guess I thought he'd give up and take it. But he didn't. He was grabbing at me, trying to get me off him while I swung my fists at his face and stuff. Then he grabbed one of my hands and started twisting it, keeping his face out of the way of my other fist. It hurt. It hurt a lot. But I kept at him, yelling at him, too. You know, stuff like, 'You don't touch her!' – that kind of thing.

Then I started feeling other hands on me. People trying to pull us apart. I could hear Murphy yelling at me to stop. Travis was there, yelling at Delilah's father, and some of the other people too. I kept feeling someone hitting me from behind. Trust a carny to kick you when you're down, I suppose. But I just tucked up my shoulders – trying to keep from getting hurt too bad – and not letting go of him. Kept trying to kick him if I could.

Finally, I got pulled off him by Murphy and Travis. As soon as they had me off him, I shook off Travis and ran for it. For a moment, I thought Murphy would chase me. But he didn't. Neither did anyone else.

I guess they all know the truth, don't they, greenie? When you're a carny, there ain't no place you can run.

CHAPTER 8

You don't need to be quiet, greenie. Come on in. I've been up and awake for quite a while now.

What am I doing? Nothing, really. Just sitting in here listening to the midway go at full speed. There's really nothing like it, you know? I've listened to it since I was little and I never get tired of it... and I hope I never do. There's just nothing like hearing the grind tapes calling people into the single-os, and the live ballys going on one after another for the live shows. Hearing the hydraulics from the rides, almost drowning out the music each of the jocks is playing to bring the rubes to his monkey box. I can hear the agents pitching their joints and under that the sound of the townies chatting each other up – all lost together in our little world for a bit, huh? And it's not just the *noises* of the lot – it's the smells, too. Hot dogs and popcorn and candy floss and other things that I'm not even sure what they are – all mixed together... something sweet... like heaven, almost.

But I'm not out there, am I? No, I'm sitting in here. Just sitting here.

This? It's a bottle. One of Charlie's, actually. Don't worry, he'll never miss it. I found it along with two other cases full of them under his bed. Being stuck in here has given me plenty of time to look around for all kinds of things. Here, pull that chair over and sit with me a bit. I happen to have this one last clean glass. Besides, if you're here, it means it's near the end of the night – because Murphy sent you to check in on me to see how I'm doing.

He always sends someone, that's how I know. Checking to make sure Charlie and I haven't gotten into it while no one else is around. So, sit down, sit down. Have a drink. I never understood before why my da liked having a bottle around... but I think I do, now. A few sips in and suddenly I can see everything in a way I never could before. The stories just keep on coming to me. And it puts me in a way that makes me not miss being out there with the rest of you. Makes being in here by myself seem not so bad. Of course, I'll feel bad when I wake up tomorrow – but what can you do?

Now, don't go telling nobody that I found Charlie's stash, all right? Seriously now. He'll figure it out soon enough, I suppose. You didn't think this was the first bottle of his I've found my way into, did you?

Ah, Murphy is good to have sent you to look in on me. I know the others have checked to see I was here – but no one ever came in to talk to me. Did I ever tell you how he came to be with the show, Murphy? No? Well then, you should definitely have a sip while we cut the jackpot! That's right! You haven't gotten to do that since you came on the road with us, have you?

It all started a long time ago – that's how all good stories start out, don't they? Anyway, I'm not sure what sent Charlie and my mum out to start a Ten-in-One show. I don't even know if my mum really had her heart set on making it happen. And Charlie being a doctor or something – it almost doesn't make sense to trade that off for the risk of a show. But, for whatever reason, they got a top, grabbed some performers, and started on the circuit to be 'with it'.

Not exactly sure how badly they were doing right from the start. But, from what Murphy has told me, in the beginning it was not going at all well. Not only were the two of them just simple Firsts of May, but I guess they brought along a green crew, too. And as for Charlie... Some of the carnies told me he thought he was just too good to listen to advice from anyone. Of course, from what I've seen of carnies and showmen, probably no one was too quick to offer any help to him, either. Gave him just enough rope to hang himself, I'll bet, and all the while keeping their eyes on the fancy equipment they hoped to buy off him cheap at the end of the season (assuming he made it that long)!

Now this whole time I'm just a babe in arms, right? Like, really a baby – in a diaper and blanket with my bottle the whole time – that's how little I am. And my mum is holding on to me while Charlie and his show have one blue date after another. Not making their nut, owing lot fees to the company running the carnival, who now won't let them leave because they owe them so much, and they're just racking up costs to add on top of it. I guess just about everyone on the circuit was figuring they'd get a piece of Charlie's show before it was all over.

So, then, about halfway through the season – and I can just see Charlie out in front doing the bally to no one on a bad spot at the end of the midway – this little guy comes up early in the day, buys a ticket and watches the grind for most of the day. Charlie thought this guy was 'kicking the tyres', that's how he put it – this little man walking around looking at everything about the show. But he didn't say anything to anyone, and Charlie tells me he wrote him off as someone looking to buy the show out or something. And Charlie says that at that point – down to a few diapers and no food coming for me anytime soon – he probably would've sold to any offer just to make it end.

Then late that night, after all the townies have gone home, Charlie and my mum are sitting at the table doing the books while I slept in a hammock nearby, when there's a knock on the door. Charlie goes and opens it, and this little man comes in – big as you please – and introduces himself as Murphy. Then, before you know it, he's sitting at the table with my folks.

Murphy once told me that he realised Charlie was chasing a dream from his childhood – something about the life caught him when he was young and never let go – like he was born with sawdust in his blood and didn't realise it until he was older.

That seems to be something Murphy can understand.

Whatever they talked about, apparently Murphy and my pops came to some sort of understanding, and my mum was all for it, too. So, as the story goes, Murphy went to the company running the carnival the next morning and had some sort of talk with them on Charlie's behalf. From that point on, the show got better spots. Not First Call, mind you – that's the best spot on the midway. No, not right off the bat, anyway – but definitely better spots than before. I guess there had never been enough room to put up the whole banner line before, and now, suddenly, they could find room for Charlie to do everything he had been trying to do. So, of course, the show started bringing in money and doing better. The season may have started out badly, but by the end of it Charlie had made enough to pay the nut and keep the show, plus a little bit to set back for the next season. During the whole down time, Murphy stayed with my folks, and he and Charlie worked on aspects of the show to build it up. Then Murphy hit the road with them again for the next season, and hasn't left Charlie's side since then.

Who was Murphy to do this? Well, if you ask him, he'll tell you he's just a simple man from a long line of tinkers. I don't even know what a tinker is. But, apparently, if he wasn't one of the original old-timers, he was brought up by one of them – Big Mike says it's almost like he's a hundred years old with all he knows, but he has the energy of a two year old. Murphy seems to know everyone, new or worn, young or old, who's on the circuit. That's why he was able to help Charlie get a fair shake from the carnival companies. Within a few years – by this point I was performing with the show, too – Murphy introduced Charlie to Big Mike, and we've been on one of his lots ever since.

Murphy taught me just about every act that I do. He taught me how to escape from a straightjacket while hanging upside down, how to tear a telephone book in half like it was nothing, and – most importantly – the skills to be a talker. He taught me other things, too: how to hang a banner line, how to be an A&S Man (the age and scale racket – you know, the game where you guess the rube's age or weight) and how to juggle the ride brake so the chumps think they're having a good time while what you're really doing is shaking the change right out of their pockets!

Not that Charlie's any slouch with that stuff either, mind you! He didn't go into this racket blind – no, sir. Murphy told me once that Charlie has more put away about the business than he could have ever known. I don't know about that – but it was Pops who taught me to breathe a fountain of flame, turn a tip, and the importance of having a shill. He's also the one who taught me to read an angry crowd to see if they're going to cause a clem – that's a big fight – and watch the weather for a blow-down. And Charlie still schools me every day in reading and maths. I couldn't check the receipts nightly if he hadn't taught me bookkeeping. Of course, right now, that's the only time we talk.

It's lonely just sitting in here, son, I'll tell you that for nothing. But that's the deal Murphy and Charlie cut with Big Mike to stay on the circuit after I mixed it up with Delilah's father in the cook shack. I guess the blame was flying around and everybody was ready to beef – but no one with any sense wants to bring in the local sheriff. After all, there are always some carnies who need to avoid the law, if they can. So I have to stay in here, separated from everyone for a bit. Charlie brings me some meals from the cook shack, or makes sure I eat from some cans here. Murphy takes time to check up on me now and again. But I haven't seen anyone else... not really.

Murphy told me that this was Big Mike's decision, because Delilah's father was bloodied up but didn't come off too badly. That's what he said, anyway... but I know he might have been hiding the truth. After all, he's the one who taught me how to fight – how to defend myself from a townie in a clem, or knock out a drunk who loses control. Besides, if I hadn't put some hurting on him, would those other carnies have jumped into the fight, sucker punching me from behind? I don't think so.

Do you like that stuff? Here, let me pour you some more. I got something else to tell you...

Just now, I lied when I told you I haven't really seen anyone else. See, being stuck in the trailer is hard for anyone – but particularly for me. I need my freedom, son, that's what I'm saying. So one night, well after the show was dark and everyone should have been done – and Charlie had been snoring away like a good drunk for nearly an hour – I snuck out to take a walk around the lot.

I swear to you, I wasn't planning any trouble. I certainly didn't want anyone to see me – I've got enough trouble as it is! So, I made sure to avoid the living lot (though, when I walked an aisle over, I saw that Mutt and Jeff seemed to be keeping watch at the gate to the back yard), and kept myself to the parking lots and front end. It was late... and I mean, *late*. Hardly a peep from anyone. So it was easy to hear the security walking their rounds of the lot, and avoid them. Well you can imagine my surprise as I was making my way back through – because I decided to make sure our banner line was still fine and can't trust Charlie to do it – and I heard voices coming from inside our joint.

Anyone else, greenie, and they never would have heard anything. But, me? I guess I was already so much on edge trying to keep from getting caught, I was paying extra attention to everything.

Now, it seemed to me that whoever was in our joint had gone to a lot of trouble not to be heard. I couldn't see any lights from inside and could only hear a murmur of voices, without being able to tell what they were saying. So I figured it was an inside job – especially if Murphy and Charlie had tied the place down like they usually do. But then I thought that if Charlie was on a tear or anything, who knows what could be going on in there?

So I snuck up, nice and quiet. A quick check of a couple of entrances showed it was tied up tight from the inside, so I went around to where I knew there was a place in the canvas that couldn't be seen from inside, and used my knife to cut a slit, big enough to let me in. I knew Charlie would be steamed about it – even if he didn't know I did it – but if something was wrong it'd be worth it. Besides, I knew it would probably be me who'd have to sew it back up.

I got inside without hearing anyone raise an alarm, and found myself just where I thought I'd be: behind some of the big wooden crates we use for storage. Now the voices were louder, I could tell there was a group of people in there, but I couldn't tell what they were talking about. Real quiet-like I snuck around the side to peak out and see what was going on.

You can imagine my surprise to see just about the whole show in there, greenie. I mean, *you* weren't there, but I could see Jerry and Travis, along with Sharon, Bettie and Abdul. I saw one of the other canvas men too, plus a couple of shadowy shapes I wasn't sure of. Maybe the half-and-half and her boyfriend or something. Like I said, I couldn't tell. They were crowded up in the pit, with just a single light in the centre of the ring, like it was a campfire they'd all sat around to sing songs or something.

And standing there in front of them was Frank. Yeah, Frank... the guy I brought in to replace Sam. He's standing there like he owns the place and he's addressing them like he's the almighty Grand Pooba of the Masonic Lodge or something. I couldn't hear much of what the others were saying – but I could hear exactly what *he* was saying.

He was saying, 'I'm just telling you, I've seen this kind of thing before. Don't forget that I've been with this show before, too. I know what Charlie is really like. I know what he's capable of doing, and you wouldn't like it if I told you the truth. And now what? We're supposed to be worried about his kid?'

There was some grumbling from the group, and it looked like Travis was arguing with someone, when Frank busted out, again, 'I'm talking about a kid who just attacks random people with no provocation. I'm talking about a kid who thinks he's running this joint, but he can't even do his own stunts without getting hurt. He goes walking around here thinking he's better than everyone else… Just like Charlie does!' Now he was getting really riled up. 'Yeah, you heard what I said. If you don't think that old Charlie Grice with his "family history with the circus" and his fancy degrees from some fancy colleges, doesn't look down on you lot, you got another thing coming!'

'You try asking him about how the show's doing,' Frank continued. 'Try asking him for an advance on your pay. Ask him if he's gonna make next week's payroll! That's how you'll get your answer, just like I did.'

That was all bull and I knew it. I overheard Charlie telling Murphy that Frank had been avoiding him for over a week – even asking someone else to pick up his pay. Murphy said he hadn't heard a peep out of him. What about you, gazoonie? You're still keeping an eye on him, right? Anything stick out to you? I didn't think so.

Then I hear Frank saying something like, 'Look – this show belongs to us as much as, if not more than, Charlie. Us! I say we demand he turn the whole thing over to us!' And after that I start to hear more yelling, like they're not all buying into what he is saying. They're starting to look restless – maybe even a little angry – so I try to back myself out of the tent as quietly as possible.

So now there is this to think about. But I'm afraid to tell Charlie or Murphy. What if they get mad at me for sneaking out, right? What if I get them in worse trouble? Besides, I don't have any proof or anything. Frank could just deny he'd said any of that. And, while some of the crew didn't seem to like what he was saying – well they *were* there listening, weren't they? And besides, not all of them *did* seem to be against him.

Go ahead and go. Thanks for listening to me – but, remember, you promised not to tell anyone about what I told you. I'll figure out what to do. I always do.

CHAPTER 9

You really had to make me look for you this time, didn't you? Look – don't worry about it, OK? I know what it's like – I've been a little bit hard to find myself, lately.

It happens right about this time on the circuit, too. The time finally comes during every tour when you're sick and tired of being stuck in with everyone else and just want some time to be on your own. It happens to everyone, greenie – even when you're not forced into hiding like I have been. But it's nice to be able to get out a bit now and then.

Oh yeah, Big Mike lifted my 'house arrest' for a bit, to see if I can 'get along' with everyone now. But Charlie won't let me back onto the stage yet. Well, maybe it's Murphy who won't. But I've been hanging around a bit, behind the scenes. You know... Just to keep an eye on things.

Look – you didn't say anything to anyone about what we talked about when you came to see me, right? Are you sure? Good.

I've been trying to keep my eye on that guy Frank. But now I can't even really bring myself to talk much to anyone in the show – all I can think about is watching them sitting around, while Frank talks to them about taking over *my* show. So now, every time I see one of them, I can hardly stand to look at them. I feel sick. It's all I can do not to spill the beans to Murphy. But how can I, when I don't have any proof?

Don't think I haven't noticed *them* looking at me out of the corners of their eyes, either. I bet they're wondering why I went after Delilah's father. Wondering why

I didn't try to sneak out and meet up with them. A year ago – maybe less – I probably would have done it, you know. Breaking curfews and sneaking out is something I've been pretty well known for around here... But now it feels like the stakes have changed. Even before Murphy pulled me aside on the midway that day to talk to me, something's been different. I don't know what, exactly. But something – oh, sorry. You want a nip? I have this... it's a flask I found in the kitchen of our trailer. Looks pretty old, huh? Don't worry, I got it cleaned out good before I dumped one of Charlie's bottles into it. It's a lot easier to carry around than a bottle!

Look – I'm not drinking a lot. Not a whole lot, anyway. Well, OK... maybe a bit more than I thought. Not that I need to, greenie, don't forget who you're talking to here! Look, this isn't what I came to talk to you about, OK? Something else happened and you are all I have, son. Pretty funny, huh? A First of May turning out to be the only person that the most 'with it' person at the carnival can talk to.

See You On The Backlot

Yeah, well... OK – it happened like this. You know how I'm not supposed to be anywhere around Delilah's joint – or anywhere on the back yard for that matter. And that's been fine, right? I mean – I was thinking that I could bide my time to get at her father. Like, he must know why I went after him, right? And so I've been playing it cool. I figure that Big Mike wants me back up on the bally as soon as I can get there. The fancy doctor that Murphy told me Big Mike was paying for has pretty much given me the go-ahead to get back up on the stage as soon as possible. But it's Charlie who's been keeping me off it. Probably been on a bender and not even realised I *can* come back, yet. Or thinks he's teaching me some sort of lesson by keeping me off it. How does he think he's going to make the nut without me?

Anyway – when there's no one under our top, I've been trying to spend time in there, checking equipment and taking a look to make sure no more accidents happen like what happened to me, right? So if Charlie makes another mistake in set-up, I should be right there to catch it.

So there I am, in the top, minding my own business. And you know what happens? All of a sudden I hear someone behind me. I turn around, afraid one of the carnies has come by to take some revenge for Delilah's father, or wants to take a poke at me for something else. Instead I turn around and it's Delilah herself, standing right there.

I'll tell you, that stopped me for a minute or two. The two of us stood there just staring at each other. Not a word for a bit. Just checking each other out.

Let me tell you what, greenie, this was the first time all season I really got a good look at her. Seeing her without the glare of the carnival's lights in the dark, without her make-up or a costume on, it kinda felt like I was seeing her for the first time.

She looked tired. Very tired. I mean just plumb worn out. She looked older than I remember her looking from last season, like there were lines around her mouth I hadn't noticed before. Her eyes seemed sunken in as though she hadn't slept for a while since being punched in the face. I always remember her hair as this wonderful deep black, but now it was ratted up a bit, like she hadn't bothered to comb it in a while. The clothes she was wearing almost didn't seem to fit her. She was wearing this skirt that hung kind of funny from her hips, and she had a jacket on over her T-shirt, but the sleeves were pushed up a bit. I could see some bruises on her arms and legs. They didn't look serious or anything. But it bothered me to see them.

It seemed like forever before she finally spoke. Her voice was quiet and deeper than I remembered. She said to me, 'I haven't seen you much this season.'

I just kinda shrugged. I mean, why would she say something like that? Of all the things for her to say to me.

'I heard about your mom,' is all I said back. 'I'm sorry.'

'Yeah,' she nodded like she understood. Then she took a few steps, like she was going to look around the top for a bit, before stopping and looking at me again. 'Why did you go after my father like that, Tony? Like that in front of everyone? It's not like you.'

'I had my reasons,' I told her, somewhat surly-like.

She took a step or two towards me. 'Like what?' she demanded. 'Come on, Tony! It's not like you and you know it. Now tell me what you were doing!'

She was getting pretty upset and I didn't want that, did I? I certainly didn't want anyone coming in and seeing us arguing. So I told her the whole thing – about the letters I'd written, my plan to see her, how Mutt and Jeff had stopped me, then how I'd snuck over the fence to get into the back yard. I even told her about being outside her window and what had happened, and then seeing her crying in the stall next to that stupid cow. Greenie, I tell you, I told her everything until I was ready to bust from the pain of it. I don't think I've ever felt anything like that before.

So she's watching me this whole time while I spill my guts out to her. And while she's looking at me, I can see that she's getting even more upset. By the time I tell her about being outside her window and how scared I was for her, I see tears start running down her face. By this point I don't know what to do, so all I *can* do is tell her everything, right? I mean, I just poured out my heart to her, right there in the sawdust under the top.

When I finish she just stands there, looking at me with tears streaming down her face. I don't even think she realised it. Like she was frozen in place, or something. Then the waterworks really start! She starts wailing out loud, running towards me. First, I'm afraid she's gonna sock me or something, so I go to step back, but I'm against the rail so I can't move. But she doesn't hit me, she just grabs hold of me tight, and won't let me go. It's like she's going to squeeze the life out of me. But I can hear her sobbing and feel her tears on my shoulder as her fingers dig into my back, you know?

I swear to you, I didn't know what to do. I mean, I've never had a girl crying on my shoulder before, you know? What am I supposed to do?

So I put my arms around her. Listening to her crying just about broke my heart, gilly. I was ready to start crying myself. Let me tell you, it was everything I wanted at that moment, to have my Delilah holding onto me, needing me. I held her as close as I could, putting one of my arms around her shoulders – you know, like you see in the movies – and telling her it will all be all right.

That just makes her cry harder, and she starts saying, 'It won't be all right! It will never be all right!' and sobbing so hard her whole body was shaking. Well, there was no keeping that quiet, was there? I knew that someone was going to hear her and come to see what was going on. But it turned out worse than I thought it would.

I look up and who do you think is standing there? Her father, that's who! Delilah's father, the man responsible for all this. But,

I guess I was just so surprised I didn't react at all. Some hero I am, huh? There she is, in my arms, practically asking me to protect her, and instead of stepping up to him I just watch as he storms in and yanks her away.

It might have been different if she'd tried to fight him off or something. That might have reminded me of what I was supposed to do. But, instead, she wraps her arms around him saying, 'Daddy... oh, Daddy,' and bawling her head off even harder. I guess that's when he sees I'm about ready to say something, because he shoots me a look, and then starts pulling her out of the tent with him. I mean, he didn't look mad or anything. Just really upset, like he was about to start crying, too.

Then I see Murphy standing at the entrance of the top. He's seeing all of this going on, but he's not saying anything. He doesn't try to stop Delilah's father as he drags her out of the joint. But he steps right back in the way of the door to keep me from leaving after them. As if that's what I was going to do! I was in no shape to go chasing Delilah and her dad down the midway anyway.

So now Murphy and I are facing off, eye-to-eye, not saying anything. I'm wondering if he's planning on trying to turn me in to Big Mike, or maybe Charlie, about all this. But he's not being quick to raise any alarm, so I decide to break the ice.

'You see all that?' I asked him. He nods to me. 'What should I do, Murphy?'

'Well, kid,' he said quietly, 'I think there is a bigger problem you and I need to talk about. Bigger than Delilah and her daddy.'

'There's nothing more important than Delilah,' I told him. He looks at me another moment, then spits into the sand and the dust in the pit.

'I'd reckoned you were going to say that,' he said, sadly. 'But there's something bigger, Tony. Leave the two of them alone for a moment, and tell me the truth.'

'Truth about what?' I demanded, getting pretty angry now.

'What is that I see in your jacket there, Tony?' he asked me, quiet-like. And I knew right away what he was talking about; this flask right here. The one in my hand right now.

'Nothing,' I told him. 'None of your business. Just something I found.'

He shook his head, sadly. 'So that's how it's going to be, is it?' he said. 'You didn't find that unless you were looking really hard. It was my gift to your da when we first met. It was full when I gave it to him.'

I listened closely. It wasn't often that Murphy talked about what it was like when he met Charlie.

Murphy continued, 'And it stayed full after our first toast until after your mum passed. I found it empty right after that. That's when I knew your da was in trouble. And now that you have it, I know that you're in trouble, too.'

'I don't know wha–,' I started to say, but Murphy interrupted.

'Don't say another word,' he yelled at me. 'This has gone on for long enough. I'm putting an end to it, Tony. An end to it, tonight!'

With no idea what he was talking about, what could I do but look at him with my mouth open?

'Don't go far, Tony,' he ordered me. 'I'm going to find your da, then the three of us are going to have a little chat and get all of this cleared out. It's going to happen tonight – and nothing is going to be the same once I've said my piece to the both of you.'

Then he stormed out of the top, practically pulling the side off of it, as one of the ties wrapped around his arm. I ran to the opening to chase after him, but he was already far away, pushing people out of his way left and right. A couple of the other folks with the show were just outside, so they probably heard what he said to me. There were some other carnies around, too, and I could see from the look in their eyes that they'd overheard everything as well.

The way a couple of them ran off when they saw me, I had no doubt that it would be all over the lot soon, too.

I felt hot and cold all at once. My face burned while my stomach felt like ice. I never wanted all these people looking at me the way they did, greenie. So I ran off, too, pushing my way through the crowd like I had a place to go to. A place I could run to and someone to back me up.

But I don't, do I? Not really. I mean, I know you like me OK, gazoonie, but I don't expect you to step into this fight that's coming. It's not yours. And Murphy knows the same thing you do, doesn't he? When you're in the carnival, there's no place else to go but the carnival is there?

Greenie, I hope you won't leave after all of this. I think you've got what it takes to be really worth it. But I don't know what will happen after tonight... after Murphy finds my pops. I don't think we will ever be the same again, just like Murphy said.

CHAPTER 10

You there, greenie? Open up!! Come on, now! I need you!!

Thank goodness. Get some clothes on and come with me. Now. Come on, there's not a moment to lose. I'll fill you in on the way to the other bunkhouse.

Look, here's what happened. About an hour ago, Murphy rounds me up along with Charlie and takes us out to one of the far parking lots — well away from the midway or the carnival — in one of the trucks, and dumps us out onto the lawn. From there we couldn't even see the lights from the living lot. There's no one around at all, it doesn't feel like the world exists any more except for the three of us out there on the crushed grass and weeds the townies park on.

I don't know what Murphy had said to Charlie before he got me there, but it must have been plenty. Charlie's eyes were red and his face pale. Whatever he was going through wasn't very pleasant.

Murphy spared nothing, 'It's time young Tony hears the truth, Charlie,' he started out. 'He needs to understand and know the real reasons why the two of you are here.'

'I know the reason why,' I interrupted, feeling angry. 'It's because Charlie drinks too much and can't run things on his own.'

If Murphy seemed shocked by what I'd just said, Charlie didn't. He seemed to know it was coming. 'No,' he started in on me, 'the problem is that you think you can run everything by yourself – but you can't! You're just a kid and you have no idea what I have to go through!'

'I know that you drink way too much and you don't have any reason to,' I yelled at him. 'You just do it so you don't have to look at me.'

'That's a lie,' Charlie hissed back at me. Then his face changed, like he'd remembered something. 'I started drinking because of what happened to your mother,' Charlie said to me. 'You just got the fallout from it.' He went to get a drink from a bottle he'd hidden in his jacket, but Murphy slapped it out of his hands.

'Tell him the whole thing, Charlie,' Murphy said with a harshness in his voice I hadn't heard before.

'He's too young,' my father started to say, but Murphy interrupted.

'He's old enough to start drinking, brother.' My pops looks stunned for a moment, so Murphy continues. 'Yeah, that's right. He's on the same path you took yourself. The one I've been trying to get you off. And what do you think he's gonna find once he gets on it? He's a man, now, whether you want to admit it or not. It's time he knows the truth.'

I look at each of them in turn. 'The truth about what?' I asked.

Murphy waited for Charlie to say something, and when Charlie didn't, he started in, 'There was an accident, see...'

'Let me tell it,' Charlie interrupted. 'Tony, I've never told you this, but it is important for you to understand. Your mother's death...' he stopped for a moment, as if to catch his breath. 'Your mother's death,' he began again, 'was an accident, just like I always told you. But... but, it was an accident that I caused.'

He took another shaky breath, but seeing that Murphy and I were not going to interrupt him, he continued. 'Your mother and I were having a fight. A horrible, terrible fight. And it was during this fight that your mother died. But it was an accident, Tony! I swear to you...'

But now I interrupted him. 'What was this fight about?' I asked, unbelieving. 'What could possibly have pushed you that far?'

'Because we found out that Frank had been...' Charlie started, then stopped. He grabbed his head in his hands for a moment like it would explode, then he burst out, 'We found out that Frank had been... sexual with you, Tony.'

I could've died right then. Just laid down and died.

'We know Frank from before, Tony,' Murphy started in. 'He used to be with the outfit... a bunch of years ago, when your da was just starting out.'

Charlie held up his hand to stop Murphy from talking more. Tears rolled down his cheeks as he reached out with both hands to me and started talking quickly.

'We had just figured out what had happened, and were trying to decide what to do. How to handle it. We were in the middle of nowhere, just yelling and screaming at each other,' he said. 'Not because we were angry at each other, but because we were beside ourselves about you! We were standing at the top of this embankment overlooking these railroad tracks.' Charlie's eyes watered as he remembered. 'I had a hold of your mother by her arms and was yelling at her, shaking her... It was so wrong, but I was just so violent in those days when I was upset. Murphy was running over to where we were. I didn't see that he was coming, but I saw your mother look at someone behind me and so I swung around ready to fight. I don't know what happened – but somehow I ended up throwing your mother to get her out of the way. Throwing her so hard that she fell down the embankment. She hit her head on the steel tracks. She was dead by the time I got down to her.'

Murphy spoke, then, while Charlie cried wordlessly. 'I saw her fall, too; there was nothing we could do. I knew it wasn't your da's fault, that it was an accident. And I made up my mind right there and then that I would stick by him and his story, even though we were afraid the law would think otherwise. When the police arrived, we told them she had just gone out walking, and when she hadn't come back we had gone out looking and found her like that. They didn't really care enough to make much of an investigation. But it was enough to worry us for a bit.'

Charlie was crying into his hands now, not looking at me. Murphy stood a bit away and, after a moment of thought, began telling me more. 'Your father's heart broke that day,' he continued. 'He's never been the same since. And not just for the death of the woman that he loved so much, the light of his life who believed in him and his love of the show and the road... but almost more so for what had happened to his son. Running the show had consumed him, had blinded him to what he should have seen happening to you. That's really when his drinking started.'

'I'm so sorry, Tony, that it happened to you,' Charlie sobbed. 'So, so sorry!'

'How could you let it?' I yelled at Charlie now, not letting him touch me. I was reeling from finding out all of this. My father was involved in my mother's death, and Frank had molested me. It was too much all in one go. Charlie fell to his knees again, his face in his hands. 'Why didn't you do anything?' I asked him.

Murphy stepped in, his hand on Charlie's shoulder. 'Do you really think he didn't?' he demanded, spitting angrily. 'For God's sake, your father was set to murder the man right then and there. Your mother, Lord knows she wanted him dead, too. But she was the clearer thinking one of the two. She wanted us to call the sheriff and get the local law on him. That's what the two of them were fighting about. It's how this horrible thing happened.'

'Why didn't you?' I asked. 'Go to the cops, I mean, when you found out?'

'Because we're carnies, you damned fool,' Murphy barked back. 'We don't get to go to the police like citizens do. You think they care about us? They don't – and especially not back in those days.' His tone softened a bit, but still held a hint of steel. 'And for something like… that. We have something of our own code here, you know,' he continued. 'We have a way of handling our own. And, trust me, that was the plan – but then this horrible accident happened with your mother, and then there was an inquest from the law… and by the time we were free and clear to put our hands on him, Frank was gone.'

I sat down, then, all the strength gone from my legs. I wanted to crawl into the ground rather than towards Charlie. 'Why didn't you say anything when he showed up on the lot after Sam's accident?' I asked. 'Why did you hire him?'

'Dammit, Tony,' Charlie burst out, 'I didn't hire him – you did!' He wiped his face off, continuing, 'Frank had already come up to me when we landed on the lot – he told me he had seen everything that happened between your mother and I, and that he knew I was responsible. And that he was going to go to the cops. He'd been in that town for a while, and he was probably a troublemaker there, too. But he'd been around them, those people, so his word would probably carry more weight than my word or Murphy's with the law. Especially considering what had actually happened. And there were just too many unanswered questions in the first place.'

'He showed up on the lot demanding I pay him to keep quiet,' Charlie continued, 'and I told him to bugger off. Then he was threatening to cause trouble at the show. It was blackmail, of course, but I figured he was bluffing and I was ready to call him on it. Then Sam gets that jolt…'

'Probably something Frank set up to happen,' interrupted Murphy. 'He always was a wily one. It could just as easily have been me, or you, Charlie, or even you, Tony, who got zapped that day.'

Charlie nodded and continued, 'And that's when Frank made his play. Like I said, I was going to call him on it, not caring what he said to anyone at that point, but then you step up and make the move to hire him.' Charlie took a breath, like he was embarrassed by the thought of what had happened. 'I thought of saying something, but having you there… seeing you talk to him… it was all too much. I just plain lost my nerve.'

'And once a part of the show, thanks to you,' Murphy said, 'Frank made good on his threats. He started demanding money from your da. Threatening to injure more people with the show if Charlie didn't pay up.'

'Still holding the threat of going to the police over my head, too,' Charlie said. 'It was just a rock, a hard place, and a fate worse than death.'

'Why didn't you fight him, Pops?' I asked Charlie.

Charlie hung his head a little shame-facedly, then, saying, 'I just couldn't. All the memories of your mother – and you – it was just easier to pay up. And when I finally started bucking him a bit – getting ready to give him the boot, and police be damned

— that's when your accident happened. I couldn't take another risk after that.'

Now it was my turn to be quiet. I guess I realised that my fire-breathing accident hadn't been because of Charlie's mistake, or mine, but because Frank was trying to get at Charlie through me. It was right then that I finally started realising what Charlie had been going through.

'I never wanted anything to happen to you, son,' Charlie was crying again. He reached for me blindly through his tears. 'I should have told you. I should have told you,' he repeated. 'But I just wanted to protect you.'

'But you didn't protect me from him in the first place,' is what I said to him then, the bitterness heavy in my voice. Suddenly, Murphy stepped up and slapped me across the mouth. He had never struck me in all the years he'd been with us – never.

'You watch yourself,' he said through clenched teeth. 'If any of us had had any idea about what he had been doing...' He left the threat unfinished. 'And ever since this bastard came on board, again, your father and I have been trying to figure out what to do. A way to get rid of him.'

'But why didn't you tell me what had happened,' I demanded from Charlie, beginning to cry a bit myself. 'Not just about Mum, but about Frank... and me... How could you not tell me?'

Charlie reached for me again... I guess to try and comfort me. But I wouldn't let it happen.

'I just thought you were so young,' he explained, 'I figured you wouldn't remember. I hoped and I prayed you wouldn't remember.' He began to sob, again. 'But I saw it in you. I saw that it had left its marks in you, Tony. Everything about the way you act just says it all to anyone who can read the signs. I tried to deny it, but I'm the one who studied psychology. I'm the one who's supposed to know and understand this stuff. And I knew, and I understood it...

and I still tried to deny it.' Charlie's tears were coming even harder now. 'I'm sorry.'

I looked at the two of them for a moment. Then I turned around and started to run for the lot.

'Where are you going?' I heard Murphy yelling after me.

I turned, only for a moment, to see Murphy trying to pull Charlie up to his feet. My pops looked more broken and defeated than I had ever seen before – but I wouldn't let myself stop. Not even for a moment.

'I'm going to find out the truth,' I yelled back at them. 'And I'm not going to stop until I get it straight from him... No matter what it takes!'

And then I ran all the way here to get you, greenie. Now I want you to come over here with me... I'm going to call out Frank. I'm going to get the truth. And I'm going to do something about it all. Stick close to me, son – it's time I set some things right.

CHAPTER 11

Are you all right? Hey! Greenie! Wake up, now – are you all right? Sit up a bit... just take it easy.

You gave us a scare, son – I'll tell you that for nothing. Do you remember what happened? Well, what do you remember? OK, OK. I got it – right? Here, let's get you up and off the midway. I'll get you a cup of coffee and then fill you in on what you missed. After all, it's important we get our stories straight in case the law comes around, asking questions.

How are you feeling now? Good. That's real good. You took a pretty good couple of knocks there, but it wasn't your fault. I appreciate that you were there. I really do. It'll be a while before Murphy and Charlie come back. Just have another cup and I'll tell you what happened after I sent you off to get Big Mike.

Well, after you ran off, I searched a couple more places and didn't make it a secret to anyone who I was looking for. Of course, I didn't say why. I was waiting for that one. I figured if I made enough noise, he'd come looking for me. And he did.

I was right in the middle of the midway's back end, walking pretty quick, right? Checking each joint as fast as I could, trying to track him down, when I heard him speak up behind me. He was saying something he must've thought was tough, like 'What do you think you're doing, kid?' or something just as dumb.

Tell you what, right then and there I made my choice. There was no way I was going to let him talk down to me, let him think for even a moment that he had some upper hand or something over me.

So I stop dead in the dust. Then I turn around nice and slow. And I'm looking at the ground when I turn, see, so I can let my eyes travel up to meet his, nice and slow – like in one of those western movies – because I'm figuring I'll show him how tough I really am with this.

But as soon as I looked at him I felt... well, I felt weak, I guess. Sick. I don't have any other word for it. Here I was, looking into the eyes of a guy who'd tried to kill me. And he did, you know. He did when he switched-out my fuels during that show, the one where I caught fire, remember? And it wasn't just that; there was also what he'd done to Charlie and my mom... and what he'd done to me. And he'd never paid for any of it.

His eyes were cold. Blue. Cold and dead, dead as the sky gets sometimes when it's lit up by the sun you can't ever see. And for a moment – just a moment – I'm thinking that I can't stand up to him.

But then I get my head on straight. I mean, this guy has been ripping us off. This guy was some kind of pervert who likes little boys. This scumbag has tried to tear my whole life apart. And the only thing coming into my head is that I need to take care of Charlie. That my pops couldn't protect me... but now *I* gotta protect him, right?

I could see from his eyes that this guy could kill me. Probably wouldn't care two shakes if he did. But I had already decided I wasn't going to let him, you know? I mean, I eat fire, right? There's no trap I can't escape from. No pain I'm afraid of, right? Nothing that worries me! And I realise that my whole life, everything I am, means that I'd rather go down fighting than just lie down and die.

All this – I mean this whole thing I'm telling you about – just happens in seconds, right? Like it's all right there in my head while we are standing there in the lights, staring each other down. I can't hear anything. I can't see anything.

It's like there's nothing else there, right? I even forgot I'd sent you off to get help. I forgot Charlie and Murphy, and the other carnies, too. There was nothing in the world but him and me, facing each other. And we were going to be playing for keeps. It felt like the fate of the world was in my hands.

So then, he's like, 'What do you want, kid?'

And I don't miss a beat, right? I answer him right back, loud and clear. 'You don't call me kid, Frank,' I told him.

I guess he didn't think I'd talk back to him like that. Maybe he thought I'd back down. And he doesn't seem to like it one bit that I'm standing up to him because it's a moment before he answers me. 'I hear you've been looking for me,' he said.

'I want the truth, Frank,' I told him, with no playing around. 'The whole thing. All of it! Everything you know.'

'Well, now,' he said, running his hand along his unshaved jaw, 'that's a lot to talk about.' He's kind of smiling now, because he thinks he has me. 'If you want to talk to me about running your show, then there's quite a bit you could learn from me, kid.'

'I'm no kid, you son of a bitch,' I spit out at him. His smile stops right there, it does. 'I want to hear what you've been saying to Charlie.'

He's not smiling now, let me tell you. 'You do, do you?' he asked me. 'Maybe you'd rather know what everyone else has been saying about your Charlie. About you and your stupid show.'

'I already know what they're saying,' I told him straight out. 'I also know that it's just what you've been telling them. And that you're a liar.' I take a breath, then, to cool down before dropping the bomb on him. 'I know you were with the show before. Charlie told me everything.'

Frank gets a little pale at this. He's

probably figuring Charlie spilled to me, and he's trying to guess exactly how much I know, right? I can see him licking his lips, getting scared. He takes a step towards me, but I stand my ground.

'Charlie tells me you've been taking money from him,' I told him. 'And that means you're robbing everyone else on the show.'

Frank spits in the dust. 'Tell you that, did he?' He was grinding his teeth. 'He also tell you I was there when he killed your momma?'

If he was trying to shock me, he was dead wrong. I could read him like I read a tip. All I had to do was push him the right way and he'd admit everything. 'He told me that's what you said,' I answered. 'But, see, I don't think you were there.' Frank's jaw stopped working.

'See, Frank,' I continued, 'I think if you'd been there, if you'd really seen something, you would have gone singing to the sheriff right off. I think you were already gone from the lot by then, because you figured out my folks knew what you'd done... to me.' Frank went even paler, if that was possible. His hands clenched into fists, knuckles white, his lips pursed into a thin line.

But I wasn't done, yet. See, my mind was racing hard. I had been wracking my brain about everything that had happened with Frank since I first saw him... and now the pieces of this puzzle were finally fitting together.

'Even if you didn't have the guts to go to the law, you would have come after Charlie a long time ago,' I said, thinking out loud, trusting in my gut that I was right. 'No, you probably heard my mum had passed on a while ago, and just played a hunch about it when you saw our show pull onto this lot. You tried to play Charlie like a rube. Then, when he didn't go for it, you rigged that accident for Sam to get yourself under our canvas.'

I figured I had just about covered it all,

so I finished big: 'You figured you'd work another angle, maybe rig some accidents, then lean on Charlie, when you figure he's weak, to start him paying you... and then you try to take the show out from under us.'

He was mad enough to kill me right then. I could see it in his face. His blue eyes blazed, his hands clenched up ready to start pounding on me.

'Bet you think you're a big man, don't you, boy?' he said with a shaking voice. 'Talking that way to me? Maybe you think your old tosspot daddy is going to be able to protect you from me?'

'I'm just saying,' I said, shrugging, 'it all makes sense. And it if makes sense to me – a kid – then I bet it makes sense to other people on the lot. Maybe even Big Mike.'

'You think they're going to listen to you?' he growled.

So help me, greenie, I actually smiled at

him right then, to drive him even more crazy. 'I think they're tired of hearing a lot out of *your* mouth,' I told him. 'I'm betting most of them will give me a good listen, and...'

Frank interrupted me, shouting, 'It won't make no difference what you say! Charlie was paying me to keep quiet about your momma getting killed.' He licked his lips, thinking hard. 'He wouldn't have done that if he hadn't had something to do with it.'

'Charlie has a conscience,' I pointed out. 'Something you wouldn't understand. He still blames himself for my mother's accident. You probably caught him on a tear, so he was feeling guilty. Anyone who knows him will understand that when I tell it.'

'You think that's going to make any difference to them?' he asked, waving behind him like he meant the rest of the carnival. 'Tell them anything you want – all that will matter to any of them is that I can make a buck. Better than you or your lousy dad!'

I'll bet he was going to leave it at that, figuring he'd won. But I had one last thing to tell him. Nice and quiet, I said, 'What if I go ahead and tell them about how you like little kids.'

'So what if you do?' he sneered back at me. 'You think they're gonna believe a little punk kid like you? You think they're gonna care what some disturbed boy says? You jumped some random guy in the cook shack! Then you make moves on his daughter! Then you pick a fight with me...'

'These people know me,' I told him. And I told him this next bit because I know that it's true. 'And they know I'd never lie about anything like that.'

'You're all liars,' he spat out at me. I can see flecks of foam flying off his lips as he begins to stagger towards me, shaking with fury. 'All you damn kids! Well, don't forget this, boy – you came on to me. Yeah, that's right – you wanted it from me! You never cried. Not once. Not any of the times I had you.'

The whole time his voice is rising. I can hear the start of a scream in his voice as he lashes into me. So, now I'm starting to feel sick. I mean, what if he's right, you know? I couldn't remember – so what if there was something to what he was saying about me? But I force myself to keep thinking about how he was trying to take the show. And I don't back off from him, even though he's staggering towards me, all crazy-like.

'Yeah!' he yelled at me, waving his hands around. 'You remember! I can see it! You know that's what you wanted.' He stumbles closer, grabbing for my shirt, but I step back, staying out of his reach.

'I'd never have you now,' he grabs for me again, but misses. He's close enough that I can smell cheap liquor on him. 'Just like no one else here would, either.'

That was when I heard you yelling, greenie. I didn't even know you were there until I saw you slam into Frank from behind and knock him to the ground. Where did you learn those moves from?

Anyway, you sure caught him by surprise – he didn't expect to find himself on the ground, that's for sure. Of course, he's a carny, ain't he? And any carny's ready for a clem, any time, drunk or not, so he was back up in a flash. You did good, though. Big Mike was telling me he thought you'd go the distance, but I guess when Frank kicked you in the knee and dropped an elbow on your melon, that was it, huh?

But you slowed him down… slowed him down good. I looked around and saw a lot of people on the midway now, standing close to us. More people than I thought worked at the whole carnival. But, I tell you, there wasn't a townie there. Or a lawman. Big Mike was the first one to speak.

'Hold on there, Frank,' I heard him yell. Lots of fat guys, they have soft voices, you know? Not Big Mike. Got a voice bigger than he is, he does.

So Big Mike's voice, booming through the midway, brings Frank up short. Instead of taking a kick at you while you were lying there all cold, or swinging on me, he looks around and sees everyone just standing there looking at him. He gets quiet too, you know? Just stands there looking at everyone, because he knows he's trapped. And the midway is quiet, too. Quiet as I've ever heard it. I didn't think it was possible for anything to be that quiet with all those people standing there.

That's when Murphy and Charlie show up. I don't know how long they'd been there. Long enough to hear what had been said, that's for sure. The circle of people standing around me and Frank parted just enough to let the two of them through – then close back up. No one was leaving here until this was all settled.

That's the carny way of life, you know. There's a beef? We keep it under our awning, if we can. We settle our own scores – and we look out for each other. Big Mike, it's his carnival, so he steps up to look over things like he's a judge in a courtroom. I just didn't know what he'd say once everything came out in the open.

'Charlie,' Big Mike asked nice and loud, 'is everything your boy says true? Has Frank here been after your stake?'

Charlie didn't say a word. He didn't need to. He just looked around at the circle of people until he was looking at Frank, then he looked at me before nodding his head slowly.

'I figured,' Big Mike said. 'Now, Frank, what have you got to say about it?' Frank opened his mouth real quick, like he was going to spout off, but Big Mike interrupts him. 'Now, I want you to think hard about what you're about to say, Frank,' he told him. 'We've had an earful already.' People around the circle nodded that they had. Some of them just stood with their arms crossed and mean looks on their faces.

Frank swallowed hard, considering his next words. Finally, he opened his mouth.

'I may have taken the chump's money,' he told the crowd, pointing at Charlie, 'but it ain't nothing compared to what he's done. It's true, I never seen his wife take that tumble, but I bet he had his hands on her when it happened – and some of you know it, too! He's lucky that that's all I did – take money from him.'

'It was an accident!' Charlie burst out.

Frank saw an opening and jumped right for it. 'Seems to me,' he yelled, 'that you're awful quick to speak up about it! You must be feeling awful guilty. Guilty for a reason!' An angry mutter went through the crowd, but I couldn't tell whose side they were on.

'Hold on, there,' Murphy interrupted, calm as can be. He stepped forward so everyone could see him, and put his hand on Charlie's shoulder. 'Now you all know me. You know who I am and where I've been. I'm telling you that I was there, and Frank was not. Charlie *was* there, but it was an accident – just like he says.' Murphy looked around the circle of people, like he was looking into each person's eyes directly. 'Most of you also know Charlie. You know his son. You know what kind of man he is.' He pointed at Frank, saying, 'And a lot of you know Frank from when he was with the show before. You know what kind of person *he* is, too.' He looked at Frank for a moment, before saying, 'And you know there's no room for a Chester here.'

You know what a 'Chester' is, don't you, greenie? It's short for 'child molester'. Charlie told me once that townies think every jock, agent and showman on the lot is a drunk, child-molesting ex-con – and while you can't argue there are certainly drunks here, you won't find much of the rest. At least, not for long. And especially with Big Mike's show – he runs a clean show through and through.

So as soon as Murphy tells everyone what he thinks of Frank, another angry mutter goes through the crowd. This one a lot darker... Everyone knows Murphy, and his word is law here and now, even more so than Big Mike's. There are always families travelling the circuit, since the joints tend to be family businesses, you know? And even if a Chester knows better than to touch a kid from the lot, no one wants a beef with the law if something happens to a local kid. It only takes once, and the whole show never works again.

Then Murphy walked over to me and told me to get you off the midway. Frank, he must've got a real lucky shot in, because you were still lying there in the dust. Murphy and I got you up and dusted you off, then I shouldered you to get you out. I saw Charlie talking quietly to Big Mike – the two of them gesturing at me. Frank just stood in the centre, giving me the evil eye.

The crowd opened up just enough for me to get you through. As I went through, I looked up to meet each person in the eye, hoping they could see the truth of what I had said. Some of them wouldn't look at me, and kept staring towards Frank. Others gave me a quick nod, and a couple of people even put their hands on my shoulder, like they were trying to tell me they understood. As we pushed our way through, they closed in tight behind us like a coffin lid.

CHAPTER 12

Hey, there! So did you get everything packed up the way it's supposed to be? The truck's in order so it can be unpacked quickly once you're on the new lot? Are you sure you pulled every dead man?

Right! Good man. I'm counting on you, OK? I need you to make sure this jump goes well.

Can you believe it? You start the season as a First of May – green help out on his first circuit – and now here you are, boss canvas man for our show! Well, it's only our top, and it ain't that big. But that's still a big leap. And you've earned it. And by earned it, I mean you really do good work... not just that you can hold your own in a clem. You're not a gilly, son, and you never were. Not from the moment you signed up with us. Lucky for me you're a good sport, huh?

Remember – you're in charge now. Well, I mean Murphy is in *charge* charge – but you've got a few people answering to you now. So don't let anyone try to send you off looking for the key to the midway, a left-handed monkey wrench or a long weight. Not unless you really just want to take a break from what you're doing, anyway. I remember one time a few years ago, I guess I was pestering Murphy while he was trying to work, because he sent me off to find the lot owner because we were out of 'light bulb grease'. Yeah, it was pretty funny. I must have spent an hour looking for the lot owner before I finally told him. Then he told me that Murphy had just sent me on a wild goose chase.

Later that season, Charlie sent me off for some 'red light bulb paint', and I ended up going to the movies! Best afternoon I ever had.

What? Oh, sure – I think this jump will go fine. What with Murphy in charge and you setting up the joint, it'll be red dates all the way, my friend!

Once you're on the lot and in the air, pay attention to your orders from Big Mike, OK? He'll tell you how the lot is running. And look out for when they pull the POP dates – that's the Pay One Price deal… like Dollar Days. Man, I hate those things. The only way you'll make the nut on those is to ding the marks as much as possible once they're on the inside. I'm saying do more than just the blade box and blow-off; do an after-catch. Use a candy pitch, sell them whatever else you need to make a buck, do whatever it takes. But remember what Charlie always says – always leave a chump a dollar for gas.

Charlie? He'll be OK. I mean – well, you know. It's been kind of difficult since we went into the programme. The one that puts us on the wagon. No drinking for either of

us. I honestly thought it would be hardest
for Charlie – he's practically been drinking
professionally my whole life! I mean, you
know, compared with Charlie, I've hardly
drank at all! You wouldn't think just...

I almost said, 'just a few weeks of
drinking'. But I can't say that. Part of
Charlie and my going into the program
together is that we have to be truthful...
to everyone. With everything that's been
happening, that's the only way we think
we can get our way through this. So, I have
to tell you that I'd been sneaking Charlie's
bottles for a while. It was just recently that
I'd gone overboard a bit. And when Charlie
and I agreed to stop – well, I guess I just
didn't think I'd have any problems. But I
was wrong. It's been a lot harder to give it
up than I expected. I guess I didn't really
understand what I wanted. Not really,
until we started the programme together.
My sponsor and I talk a lot – not just about
my wanting a nip now and then – but about
what it was like living with Charlie and his
drinking. This guy, my sponsor, he's been
telling me about how with some people,

needing to drink runs in their families. I'd never thought of that before.

So it looks like the programme will do us some good, you know. But it'll be tough, being on the circuit and not drinking. They go together like... um... I don't know. Maybe they actually don't, and I've just wanted to see it that way.

Honestly, I'm more worried about how Charlie will do in jail. I mean, I don't know for sure that he's going to jail, but we're both kind of worried about it. More than just the two of us, because I know that Big Mike is worried, and Murphy is worried. You're probably a little worried, too, huh? But it will all be OK.

Charlie and I talked a lot about it, you know. When we left the show for that couple of days, it was because he took me to the spot where it happened. To where my mother fell onto the tracks that night. I don't know what I was expecting, really... old, dark forest and stuff, I suppose. But when we get there, it turns out they've built housing developments all over it. The train tracks she fell on aren't even there any more. Charlie explained everything that happened to me – explained it until he was shaking with sobs again.

And, for a while, I cried with him...

Murphy is the one who drove us there. Then the three of us had a sit-down to decide what to do next. Murphy and I both agreed with Charlie that he should turn himself in to the law. It was tough to decide on, but we all agreed that his guilt was killing him and that the only way he was going to get himself together was if he really felt he had confessed everything to someone.

I guess that night he and Murphy called Big Mike, because the next morning he showed up at the motel we stayed in. Then all four of us walked into the sheriff's office together and Charlie asked to speak to a detective. I don't know who this guy was, but he seemed to know all of us. Big Mike told me later that he was the original detective who'd investigated my mother's accident.

See You On The Backlot

This detective was pretty sharp. I could see it in his eyes when he looked us over. What's more, he didn't look very surprised to see Charlie standing there, saying he needed to talk about my mother's death. If he was surprised at anything, it was when Pops explained to him who I was. But even then, he kept pretty cool about it, I'll give him that.

So this detective, he calls in a couple of other lawmen and they pull Charlie into a room to take a statement from him. I guess Big Mike was there to sort of act as a lawyer for him. I think that's what he was there for anyway, because he stayed close to Charlie the whole time. Murphy told me to have a seat while some other detectives sat him at a desk to take his statement as a witness.

I've spent my life trying to avoid the police, you know – and now here I was, sitting in the middle of Johnny Law's house, trying to look inconspicuous. But the people at the station were OK to me. Someone brought me a soda and put me in a waiting room with a couch so I could be comfortable while I waited.

178

Not sure how long I was there before the sharp detective came to find me. He walked in and shut the door behind him so it was just the two of us. I was kind of scared, then. I mean, I was afraid I'd say the wrong thing and make it worse for Charlie or something. Maybe get Murphy and Big Mike in trouble, too. So I just kind of looked at him while he pulled up a chair and sat down in front of me.

'So you're Tony, huh?' he asked me, patting his pockets like he was looking for a cigarette… then stops and looks frustrated for a moment when he can't find any. 'You were a lot smaller when we met twelve years ago.'

'Yeah,' I said, ' I grew up.' I wasn't trying to be a smartass or anything… it just kind of slipped. I felt lucky when he smiled a little bit at what I'd said.

'Got a son, myself,' he told me, friendly-like, 'about your age. Thinks he knows everything, too.'

I'm not interested in games with him, so the next thing out of my mouth is, 'What's going to happen to Charlie?'

This detective, he sighs and leans forward so his face is up close to mine. 'You're a lot more hard-boiled than my boy is, Tony,' he said to me, quiet and serious. I can see from the look in his eye he's wishing he had a cigarette. 'I'll get right to it, then. Your father will probably be OK. When he told us he wasn't there, when I originally investigated your mother's death, well... that didn't seem to add up. But he says it was an accident, and the evidence pretty much backs him up. What he just told me answers some questions I had.'

He sat back, then, loosening his tie and running his hand through his hair. 'It doesn't hurt that that guy Murphy backed up Charlie's version exactly, and offered to be a witness. Between him and the guy who runs the carnival...' He let his voice fade, leaving his sentence unfinished. 'There will be a formal investigation,' he said after a moment, looking closely at me, 'and that may end up in a court hearing or some such. We'll just have to see. The case has been listed as unsolved, and I really never thought it was a murder – but this may help us to close it finally.'

I felt a huge relief, like a big weight was off my shoulders, when the detective said it was probably taken care of. But I stopped breathing for a moment when he said the word 'murder'. Probably wasn't until that moment that it occurred to me just how serious this whole thing could have become.

After a moment, the detective leaned in to me again. 'Tony,' he started, 'there's something else.' I looked at him nice and calm, wondering what he wanted.

'I want to know what happened to Frank,' he said to me.

Well, you could have knocked me over right then, let me tell you. If there was something I didn't expect, this was it. 'I don't know what you mean,' I told him, looking him in the eyes and trying to be cool.

He looked directly into *my* eyes, before continuing. 'Yeah?' he said. 'See, your father mentioned that an old crew member, Frank, had been threatening him. That's why he came forward. Guilt and that kind of thing.' The detective rubbed his chin, thoughtfully, like he was waiting to see how I'd react. 'But now, no one seems to know where this guy is. Not your father. Neither of the other guys. In fact, while you've all been here, we had the State Troopers go and enquire at your carnival. No one seems to know anything.' He was looking at me hard when he asked, 'You know where this guy is, Tony?'

Well I mean, I don't know what happened to Frank. How could I? After I pulled you off the midway to clean you up, I don't know what happened. I didn't hear anything else about it, and didn't see him again. Even when I asked Murphy about it later, all he would say is that Frank was 'taken care of'. So I tell the detective the entire story about my face-off with Frank on the midway, answering his questions when he has them, then I finish it by telling him, 'I figured the lot gave him the DQ.'

'DQ?' he asked me, a little rough. 'What's a DQ?'

I shrug and told him, 'It means we kick him off the lot. Out of the carnival. For good. I think it's short for *disqualified* or something... that's what Murphy told me. Anyway, when a yokel gets rowdy, or we find a carny who's been causing problems, he gets the old DQ. Do you know what I mean?'

This detective, he looks into my eyes, right? Like he can see into my soul or something to see if I'm telling the truth. But what can I do? I just keep looking at him... willing him to believe what I'm saying, because I don't know what else I can say.

Then I guess he did believe me, because he runs his hand through his hair again and stands up, straightening his suit. 'OK. OK, I got it,' he said. Then he turns to me before he heads out the door. 'Look, Tony,' he said, 'you're not in any trouble. And your father isn't a suspect or anything. We're not going to put him in jail or anything at this point. But he has to stay in town until we finish our investigation. Now, I talked it over with the carnival owner – he's willing to take responsibility for you, with your father's permission, if you want to head out. It's your choice.'

I sat for a moment, thinking about it. 'What would you do?' I asked him.

He stopped in the doorway for a moment, then he told me, 'I know I'd want my son to be with me, if I was in a position like his.' Then he left me there.

So that's why I made the decision I did.

I'll be OK. But I had that choice, of whether or not to go with the show… but I want to stay with Charlie for a bit. Family first. I mean, everyone in the show is family too, really. But that's why Murphy and I arranged all of this with Big Mike. To take care of all of you. Luckily, with your help, the rest of the crew came on deck – even though the half-and-half's boyfriend didn't seem too thrilled with his new job. But I don't care about him. You don't either, do you? Good – he's not worth it.

Let's not worry about it right now. Just look to the jump to the next lot, and make sure it goes the way it's supposed to. Here, I've got a couple things for you.

Now, just in case this jump goes a little long, make sure you have some beans for the rest of the crew if they start showing some wear. Jackie – that wiry little jock who runs the chump twister – he usually has a supply, and the price isn't bad. Those little bop pills have gotten us through some tough runs until everyone can get some rest. And make sure none of the forty-miler cake-eaters sees you have them. And don't try to get them from anyone you don't know! You don't want to bring the law down on you.

Murphy will be handling most of the payroll and other money stuff, since he's in charge. You know to check in with him about any questions you might have. But, just in case you need to do it, remember not to pass out too much of a draw to the crew after you drop the awnings at night, or they'll show up drunk the next night... assuming they show up at all!

All right. Looks like you are ready to go. I'll catch up with you in a few days. Keep all the wheels on the ground, the road under you and the red ones each night. I'll see you on the backlot.

CHAPTER 13

Found me, did you? You look like you're ready to cut the jackpot with me, so things must have been going well.

Another red date, son, the way it is supposed to be. Blue dates may come and go, but a red date makes up for every single one of the blue ones, doesn't it? Now, remember what I told you, once you have a buck in your kick, you want to keep it there! Stay out of the G-Top until you have more than a circuit under your belt. They'll take everything you got without a second thought. When you get a big roll – and I'm not talking about a carny roll, mind you – that's something you'll want to hold onto. Once you've got something big, you might want to think about retiring. Or getting your own place... even your own top, maybe. You could run a single-o, like Delilah's father.

Oh, did I tell you he came and talked to me? Delilah's father, I mean.

Yeah – I was surprised, too. It was the day after I got back on the lot. I was making my way over to that new single-o that Big Mike put on the back end while we were gone. You know the one: the new question mark show. Yes, you've seen it. It's just a small joint, has a big sign that says, 'What is it?' in big letters out front. They are saying it's a Missouri McCurdy Mummy, or something equally gruesome. That's what some of the carnies are saying it is, anyway, and they all seem to be getting a good laugh out of it. It's got to be a gaff. But what could it be made of? And I don't know whose joint it is. It doesn't much matter, I suppose.

Anyway, I was heading over to see it, and he steps right out in front of me, big as you please. I figure he's there to demand I apologise for taking a poke at him that day in the cook shack. Especially since I've been going around and apologising to just about everyone for acting so badly lately. Of course, I've been avoiding him because of what I thought he'd done to Delilah.

But, see, he steps up to me, and asks me to take a moment with him, all polite-like. I wasn't expecting that, tell you that for nothing, but I said, 'OK.'

So we step off the midway towards the back yard and he told me, 'Delilah thinks a lot of you, Tony. I'm guessing that's why I found her with you that day.'

I just nod to him, so he fumbles for the words a bit, before he says, 'I know you two used to be close, but it hasn't been that way lately.' Then he asked me to sit down on the back of a truck with him, so he can talk to me more. 'Delilah's been having some trouble lately, Tony. I don't mind telling you that after her mom passed... well... it's been difficult...'

'Well,' I interrupted him, 'she can come to me any time. You know, to talk.' He just looks at me, so I added, 'With your permission, sir.'

He looks at me funny a bit more, and then said, 'I'm sure she appreciates that Tony, but I don't think you understand what I'm getting at. Let me ask you this: when you jumped me that day, in front of everyone, you kept saying something about Delilah, right?' I nodded, so he continued. 'So you were the one outside our trailer that night? The one who ran off, then? You do know what I'm talking about, right?' I nodded again, slowly. He sighed, heavily.

'Tony,' he started, 'I was the one who chased you off. I thought you were in on it.'

'In on what?' I asked.

He sighs again, like he's trying to figure out an explanation, then he said, 'Delilah had starting acting out. She was upset about her mom passing. It was cancer. It had been coming for a while – and her mom and me, well, we tried to keep Delilah from knowing. So when her mom died, I think she blamed me a little. Anyway, once we got on the circuit for this season, Delilah started hanging around with some of the carnies that I don't like. And started getting into some bad things.'

He looked at me to see if I understood. I nodded, so he said, 'It took a bit – I mean, I was pretty busted up about her mom, too – but it finally got through my thick skull that she was doing drugs.' He looked really sad and upset. 'I would have figured it out earlier; you know we see things like that all the time. But I couldn't figure out where she was getting the money for it, right?'

I nodded again. Everyone on the lot has heard stories about someone on drugs doing a hold out from the receipts, or stealing money in order to keep their habit up. Even my sponsor and I talked about it as part of the programme.

'I'm sorry, Tony,' he told me, 'you may

not want to hear this, but it's important you know. Some of the carnies were... giving her ways to make money that weren't... well, they were using her pretty badly, Tony. I just think you ought to know – as her friend.'

Suddenly, those puzzle pieces with Delilah's picture on them that'd been jumbling around in my head finally clicked into place. Those two, Mutt and Jeff, hanging around and keeping me from talking to Delilah. The sounds I'd heard inside the trailer. The way she looked and acted to me that day. I felt my face flush hot, and my stomach turn to ice. Honestly, I felt like the world's biggest chump right then. Delilah's dad, I guess he could tell, because he put his hand on my shoulder.

'Don't blame yourself,' he told me. 'She was just lost for a bit there. I actually have you to thank for turning her around. After she talked to you that day, she told me everything that had been going on. I... I was able to get her some help. Finally.' He rubbed his eyes for a minute, like they were bothering him, before continuing. 'I have some family up north. She's staying with them for a bit while I wrap up this season. After that, we're going to figure out what to do.'

I could see he was pretty upset, but that it was important to him that I understood. I felt bad for Delilah and her father. I felt bad that I'd blamed him for what was happening to her.

'Will I get to see her?' I asked him.

He shrugged. 'Probably not,' he told me. 'But you can write to her if you want. I hope you'll let her know you want her to get better. Just get the letters to me, and I'll make sure she gets them.'

I nodded to him. 'Yeah,' I said, 'I'd like that.' Then we both stood up and shook hands, really somber. It really felt like he'd done something important, telling me what he had. Then he went his way, and I went mine. I have a few letters already, for him to give to her. Then a few more, too, after that.

Which reminds me; have you seen Mutt or Jeff, lately? No? Me, neither. I asked around a little bit, but no one was interested in talking about them. That's what happens when the goon squad gives you the DQ, my friend. It's like you never existed!

Where do you think Frank went? Oh, I don't think he went too far. That McCurdy Mummy had to come from somewhere, right? He won't be missed. Leastways, not by anyone here.

Well, like I told you when we met, we do right by the other people on the lot, and they do right by us. And you better, too, if you're going to be on the road, whether you're with us or not.

No, I'm not saying we won't be on the circuit next year. But, right now, it's hard to say.

I mean, I'm no punk kid, right? I've spent all these years with the show, being the 'Clown Prince of Sideshow' for everyone, both the chumps and the carnival folks. Not afraid to take a hayseed for everything he's got – while always leaving a mooch a dollar for gas – and ready to wow the ladies right out of their panties, too. The guys, they've always got a girl show to go to, but the dames – well, they have me, don't they?

Look, you're educated now. You're with it. You understand how the carnival works, so no one can take advantage of you. And you can help watch everyone else's back, too. As I've always said, this is our world! From one end of the midway to the other, through the backlot and back yard, front end to back end. Rides, games, shows, single-os, grease joints... each and every single agent, pitchman, talker, jock, freak and act, working to make their nut to stay on the road. And I've never really considered any place else for Charlie and me but the road. Never really considered another place for us to go. Much less thought about another way for us to make money.

I mean, what else could we do? Go

straight?

But Charlie, he's a smart man. That's part of what helped him during the inquest. College degrees and fancy writings – maybe that's what he should be doing, instead of being on a bally stage trying to turn a tip. And me? I don't think there's any place I couldn't fit in if I didn't want to. It made me think of something Murphy once told me. It went something like this:

'Kid,' he said – he's the only one I ever let call me 'kid', like I've told you before – 'a lot of folks on the lot, they live in their own little world – and they can never get beyond it. Their life starts and ends between the front end and back end. The problem is, there's a much bigger world out there. And our carnival is just a tiny little piece of that big huge thing, not the other way around. But you? You're smart enough so that you can understand that. And what's more, you can be understood by all sides, too, if you really want to. The carnies, they know you and respect you. And put you out with the citizens?

Well, they can understand and respect you, too, if you let them. That is an important skill, kid – and it will take you far.'

I still remember the look in his eyes when he said, 'But you have to get out there and do it. If you stay here, you're limiting yourself. If you really want to make something of yourself, then there has to be more to you than being on the backlot.'

So that's what I've been thinking about. Whether or not I can really get out there and make something of myself beyond this canvas top. And I think I can...

But let's face it, gazoonie, I'm not in a hurry to get to it today! Right now, I can smell money in the pocket of a mark from a mile away, even over the popcorn and candy floss of the midway. I can hear change jingling in a hayseed's pocket under the sound of a ride that's there just to shake it loose. I can hear the townies' shoes walking along the sawdust of the midway, and feel the buzz of their voices as they look at the banner lines, marvelling at the acts waiting for them inside. I can imagine their dreams, and I'm ready to make them come true under our top.

Come on. It's time to start the bally.

Bone Song
SHERRYL CLARK
Melissa is running scared... and she daren't make friends or tell anyone her secret.

Breaking Dawn
DONNA SHELTON
Is friendship forever? Secrets, betrayal, remorse and suicide.

Don't Even Think It
HELEN ORME
One family's terrible secret.

Gun Dog
PETER LANCETT
Does having a gun make you someone? Does it make you strong or does it actually make you weak? Stevie is about to find out.

Marty's Diary
FRANCES CROSS
How to handle step-parents.

Seeing Red
PETER LANCETT
The pain and the pleasure of self-harm.

Stained
JOANNE HICHENS
Crystal is a teenage mum in despair. Can't anyone see the tragedy unfolding? Her only hope is Grace next door.

The Finer Points of Becoming Machine
EMILY ANDREWS
Emma is a mess, like her suicide attempt, but everyone wants her to get better, don't they?

The Only Brother
CAIAS WARD
Sibling rivalry doesn't end at the grave – Andrew is still angry with his only brother, so angry he's hitting out at everyone, including his dad.

The Questions Within
TERESA SCHAEFFER
Scared to be gay?

Ransom